SIGHT OF
ENDEAVOUR

SIGHT OF
ENDEAVOUR

T.A. DEANE

Book One of the Endeavour Series

PREFACE

Sight of Endeavour, and the series of books which follow it, came into being as a way of visualising, and testing out, how an idea I had for a business would work in reality. Doing that necessitated the creation of actors, and then the casting of ideas from my mind to those characters. From there a plot, and subplots emerged, the themes for which explore the untapped power of knowledge, individuality, going deep into the meaning of value, and why it is that understanding one's own value in one's personal, professional, and business life, merits time and effort. I did not anticipate writing even a single book on the matter, not to mind a series of them, because I did not anticipate having the inclination to keep going, and finish writing. The definition of endeavour is to try hard to do or achieve something, and while I have managed to achieve far more than I had ever set out to, I have above all managed to prove myself wrong, which, again, signals the importance of my earlier statement, that understanding one's own value merits time and effort.

May you, wonderful reader, enjoy your own endeavour, whatever form it takes and whatever it means to you, and may you smile at the sight, every step you take towards your own Endeavour.

ACKNOWLEDGEMENTS

Thank you to all of my family and my dear friends, near and far, for all your words of support and encouragement. To my wonderful proof-reading draft checker team, thank you from the bottom of my huge heart. To James, Stefan, and the wonderful team at Spiffing Publishing for the incredible cover design, the support and care you all showed toward this author, I am forever grateful to you.

To Stephen, my wise and precious superman, the most perfect cure to writers' block that I could ever have asked for, I thank you. In the very moment that we met; two worlds collided to become one. I loved you then, for taking my hand in yours to explore our new world together. I love you, now, for the way that, you, and I, have made that world ours.

CHAPTER ONE - INSIGHT

"Swibble," Charlie Rochford said, taking in the sight of his magnificent face, her fingers interlocked with his, her blue eyes sparkling with laughter, in anticipation of his response.

"What on earth do you mean this time?" he asked and smiled, revelling in the way that her head lay nestled on his chest, and as he felt the lasting vibration of the word she spoke, deep within him.

"It is a new word I invented," she answered.

"All words are invented." His smile broadened as he continued, "And though we have had this same conversation hundreds of times, I have to wonder what it is that swibble could possibly mean?"

"Well," she said, "squabble means to engage in a petty quarrel over something trivial, and squibble, according to urban slang, is defined as that little shaking motion made with one's hips when one is happy or snuggly. Then 'swibble' is to describe situations which may be trivial and unimportant to others, even to you, but makes me happy and snuggly, and wanting to shake my hips."

She saw a shadow of question cross his face, then the thrill she always felt from the way his face lit up, his dark, ocean blue eyes meeting hers. Kissing her forehead gently, he declared, "Happy birthday, Charlie, my darling, and I, Michael Weston, am swibble, a word, my love, that I will gladly add to the dictionary of you and I."

She moved ever so slightly, raised her head from his chest to bring his mouth closer, delicately planted a butterfly kiss on his lips, and said, "To you, my love, to the day I met you to now, for all that we have accomplished together and separately, happy anniversary, and I, Charlotte Rochford Weston, am swibble."

Finding her soft, sensual lips again, he lost himself in the touch and sensation of her, and she of him. Delicately, he moved her slim, soft body onto his, and in the rising light of a new day, they found beautiful, slow tender, sensual, ecstatic union in one another.

Later, as he sipped the coffee which she had made for them, he watched her dress for the day ahead as the chief of her own company, Endeavour. He was seeing the image in his mind of what he would paint that day. It was of her; it was always her and had been from the moment he had met her. It would be his gift to her. To, and for, his love of her. An expression of what he had felt that morning when he had run his strong hands up and down the curvature of her spine. The way it moved as she did, the softness of her skin beneath his fingertips. So close, the way her hands reached back for his, fingers interlocking at the moment when he felt her body tense, then they both shuddered in beautiful, harmonious release. He had taken in her face; it was the touch of her that he vividly recalled.

He told her about it, her eyes looking at him in the reflection of the mirror, as she deftly put last touches to her makeup.

She always savoured the sight of him, as he described a painting that he had not even created yet. It was as if he were talking to himself, cycling through the colour palette, the shadows and lighting, the brushstrokes he would use to fill the canvas. Slipping on her heeled pumps and her navy suit jacket, she went to him, kissed the top of his head, kissed his lips, then pulled him to his feet and said, "I love you, Michael Weston, go paint her!"

****

As Charlie pulled into the car park, she proudly took in the reflected sunlight on the tall, glass-enclosed, custom-built headquarters of her company Endeavour, and she thought of Michael. The memory of the morning with him made her glow. Their days and nights, and now their years together, being with him had that effect on her, smiling at the knowledge, delighting in the pleasure of it.

"Good morning, Sara," she said as she stopped to talk to the hardworking and purpose driven young woman, whom Endeavour had employed five months ago as front office administrator.

Charlie reviewed the client, visitor, delivery, security and maintenance schedules for the day and week ahead, and with Sara deftly making adjustments, they identified potential issues, overlaps, and busy periods when Sara might need support. The naturally efficient, methodical way in which Sara worked, and her cheerful disposition had made an impression on everyone at Endeavour. Those who watched her work saw that she thrived on it, and in such a short time, she had made the front office operations entirely her own, improving multiple aspects of how it was managed and run. Sara would soon be moving into a new position, and they were already beginning to train a new administrator.

"Wonderful, all our new people have arrived. A fun new day and journey in store," Charlie commented.

"Yes, they are settling into room one. Peggy and her group are in room two. Amy in room three, with Jane in room four."

"Thank you, Sara, and remember who it is you are working for and that who is you, not me," she said as she walked away from reception toward the training suites.

"You too, Charlie," Sara said, as she watched the back of the elegant woman walk away from her.

Sara had worked in many temporary jobs as she put herself through school and then university for her corporate law degree. She had read about Endeavour, had seen Charlie on the cover of magazines, in news feeds and newspapers, and had studied everything she could find but had never dreamed of meeting her, never mind working with her. She recalled the occasion, five months ago at the university, following a talk on business and economics which Charlie had given, that she had first met Charlie in person.

The talk which Charlie had given was, to Sara, inspirational, astute and unlike anything she had heard or read before. The highlight for Sara, which had the deepest impact for her was when Charlie, in response to a question from the audience said, "My business, indeed any business, big or small, new, or well established, is not a charity. I do not work solely for my community, nor for the direct benefit of others. I work for myself to make a profit. A profit in terms of wealth yes, but also that which I gain in terms of knowledge, and the enjoyment which I derive from my own achievement towards my own goal, which is to accumulate a profit, which then I can disburse or reinvest, in others or myself, as I see fit. Achieving a profit is not automatic. It is, however, the outcome of years spent visualising and testing problems, solutions, concepts, ideas, and my own capacity to think, to do, to enact and bring them to life. That the business which I run makes a profit means that the talented, driven, self-motivated people who work with me at Endeavour, also profit. They work with me, not for me, and do so for their own profit and benefit. I am neither a master nor a slave. I do not care to work with anyone who wants to be my master, or my slave. It is probable that my way, the Endeavour way, of working does benefit the community. Is this perhaps a by-product of the business? Yes, but it is not the goal. Do I believe that the public, the wider community is entitled to a share of the profit in my business without having to do anything to earn it? No, I do not. That is what tax is supposed to be for though if I had my way, I would stop the farce that has become the tax system, which serves no one's interests, except those who work in the industry, which has been created around it."

As Charlie had articulated her response, Sara heard many gasps and murmurs from the audience and watched as many of them stood up and left. That Charlie was not perturbed by the exodus was a source of deep admiration in Sara.

She had to find an opportunity to meet Charlie, and as she mingled with the audience afterward, she took it. Slightly nervous about what to say, she approached Charlie, who was politely discussing a point of economics with a group of business majors. Sara fumbled out the words, "I want to come and work for you."

Charlie, with a grateful expression and graceful motion, stepped away from the students, fixed her piercing blue eyes on the young woman in front of her, and asked, "Who are you, do you, and are you sure?"

"I am Sara Goodwin, I want to work with you, not for you, and yes, I am sure."

"I am Charlie Rochford. You understood the subject of my talk then."

"Yes."

"Did you understand why people in the audience left, as I answered that question posed to me?"

"Yes."

"Why did you choose to stay and not leave too?"

"Because even if I thought your statement was incorrect, if I were to merely gasp at hearing it, to then stand up and walk out, as if in some form of silent protest, is, to my mind, an exercise in futility. It is an attempt to negate your freedom to speak for yourself but achieves very little in the long run. Far more can be achieved by staying, by asking questions, and by challenging precisely what you said, not challenging your right to think or say it. I chose to stay because I saw no reason to leave and furthermore, I agree with you."

"What are you studying here at the university?"

"In my final year for a corporate law and economics degree."

"Good. Well then, Sara Goodwin, today is Wednesday, come to see me, Endeavour headquarters, nine o'clock Friday morning."

As Charlie spoke, she took out her phone, took Sara's phone number and details, made an adjustment to her calendar, and sent a brief message to the administrative team, the finance, legal and talent chiefs, and she added, "The team will be expecting you. You will be there all day, be prepared for that. We do not follow what you might consider to be normal candidate recruitment or selection practices, we work quite differently, which may not be familiar to you, so be prepared for that too."

"Thank you, Charlie, I will be there," Sara answered excitedly.

Sara had walked through the doors of Endeavour for the first time at eight-thirty on that next Friday morning. While she had no idea of what to expect from the day ahead, she knew that she would be very content to walk through the doors of Endeavour, every day, for the rest of her life, and for no other reason than to take in the sight of it, the vast lobby, tiers of floors stacked above her, with natural light that poured in from all sides and above. The building, it seemed to her, not only held life within it, but was a living, breathing structure all of its own. As she walked toward the reception desk, she heard the faint hum of voices, the fragrant aroma of freshly brewed coffee in the air.

"Good morning, I am Sara Goodwin. I have a nine o'clock appointment with Ms Rochford."

"Good morning, Sara. Welcome to Endeavour. My name is Adam, and I have been expecting you. That you are here early is wonderful. Here is the digital visitors' log, we will get you signed in, and settled in with tea or coffee, and then set you up with me here at reception. You will meet many people today, which I know can be overwhelming, so to help you out with that, I will show you our 'who is who' mugshot list, which David Banner, the chief of talent, named."

It had occurred to Sara, many times, when she thought back to her first encounter with Charlie, then with Adam, and over the course of that first day, what was so very different about Endeavour in comparison to where she had worked previously. On both occasions, she was presented with a decision: to act or not act, and which to do was her choice alone to make. To come to Endeavour, or not. To begin to learn and work with Adam, or not. She recalled the ease that she had felt with everyone she had met right across the company. People worked as a coordinated and connected team, but it was the power of individual action, individual responsibility and accountability which made that coordination possible. Each knew their individual purpose within Endeavour, and understood how their purpose, their role was in turn enabling and powering other parts of the business. Each person displayed pride and pleasure in how they worked, and why. There was not a single rumbling of complaint from the people she met about the company or how it operated, nor was there an expectation of a larger share of the company's profits, because the responsibility for running the entire business was not entirely theirs; it sat with Charlie and the management team. That day was, by her previous experience and as Charlie had also foretold, unusual; however, Sara soon discovered that the way in which people worked at Endeavour was entirely natural. Endeavour, she thought, embodied in clear, concrete terms, what could be achieved from a different way of thinking about a business, from seeing people as individuals, and not as a collective mass of bodies that require control because they were unable to think, or do for themselves. She had firmly understood why Charlie was, in every sense of the word, successful, and why Endeavour was designed the way it was.

Sara was sprung from her reverie by the ringing phone on the desk, as she glimpsed Charlie disappear through the doors to the training suite and with her customary bright, cheerful smile, seeing the number on the display Sara answered the phone and said, "Good morning, David, how may I help you?"

Listening to his answer, she replied, "Yes, she is, and on her way to training. Yes, I saw the order, I will put them on her desk when they arrive this afternoon."

As Charlie walked down the long corridor toward the training rooms, she sent a message to Michael saying, 'I look forward to meeting her! Swibble (smiley face). See you tonight.'

Through the mellow, drifting sound of a Ms Skyrym playlist, Michael, heard his phone pinging on the stand beside him, and knew without looking who it was from. He felt her, deeply connected to her, even when she had been thousands of miles away from him.

Reaching for his phone, his eyes leapt to the pencil sketch he had started when Charlie had left earlier that morning. He saw the delicate contours of her back, the intricate, intimate positioning of both their hands emerging from that beautiful place in his mind, onto the paper.

Smiling, he replied, 'She is beautiful. Ready for canvas, going to the studio. See you, beautiful.'

Michael stood, and stretched his tall, lean body. Carefully handling the sketch, he removed it from the stand, and walked to his studio, nestled in the garden at the back of the house. His eyes landed on the sight of blooming trees and spring flowers that Charlie had lovingly planted many years before. He loved his work, putting brush and colour to canvas, bringing the scenes he saw in his mind and around him to life. Inasmuch as she adored his work, he adored her, the entirety of her, and the way in which she saw the world, expressed so beautifully here before him as a canvas of colour, texture and fragrance, of real and beautiful nature.

Turning on the coffee machine, he chose a canvas, placed it on one easel, the sketch on the other. As he selected his colours, he thought of his life before Charlie. He recalled his two ex-wives, Ingrid, and Annabel, then his divorces from them. He thought about how once upon a time, he had thought finalising both divorces were two of the happiest days of his life, and then he met Charlie, which had put a whole new meaning to the word happy.

He thought of his work in banking, first as a teller, then to his slow progression through the ranks to become manager, and eventually president of Capital Enterprise Bank. As much as he had an eye for detail in art, he also had an eye for detail in credit applications, mortgages, and investments. He had thoroughly enjoyed his career in banking but what he was doing now, painting and creating, had been his passion right throughout his life, and he had no intention of stopping, the passion for his work was his motivation, powering him forward.

Though painting was his passion, the harsh reality of being an artist, even one with a fine arts degree as he had, was that doing what he truly loved was one thing, making a living at it, was something else. To pay bills, rent, to buy materials, just to live, he needed a job. Back then, the bank was hiring so he applied and got a job. On the day he joined the bank, he promised to never leave his true passion behind; he recalled with pride, as he looked around his studio, and thought of his gallery which now housed paintings that he had completed across the decades, that he had not.

Sitting in front of the canvas, the pride he felt washed over him. The pleasure of it, combined with the knowledge of what it was he was about to paint – he found himself swibbling. He laughed to himself, and smiled as he picked up his brush, and then he began to paint her.

CHAPTER TWO - INNER SIGHT

As Charlie approached, the automated doors opened to bring her into the training suite lobby to four state of the art training rooms. As she stepped into room one, she took in the sight of the twelve women and men who awaited her, each person seated at workspaces that were arranged in a circular cluster, her workspace was positioned in the centre. She had spoken to each member of the group several times, she knew their names, backgrounds, why they were here and what they were looking to accomplish in their roles within Endeavour Operations. Seeing her, the chief of the company, about to deliver first day training to them was a common, natural event within the world of Endeavour. Based upon her own experience from the outside, it was quite an unnatural and foreign occurrence to have the head of a company delivering training to new people, but she gave no unnecessary thought to that because she was no stranger to hearing her ideas described as, 'unnatural', 'foreign' or 'impossible'.

Charlie had really struggled, from quite an early age, to comprehend why it was that a thought or idea expressed by her, or indeed anyone, could be described as impossible without any curious exploration or questioning of the idea first. She thought it was perhaps possible that others were simply not as curious as she, but over time, despite repeated effort to change how she spoke about her ideas to pique curiosity, she found there was something else which she had yet to grasp. As it seemed that what she needed to grasp was outside her reach of comprehension, it eventually became easier for her to not say anything, instead for people to think her quiet, shy, introverted and even rebellious but all the while she was observing, learning, developing an understanding, and then examining her understanding, her learnings, and observations.

Over the years, she had discovered that it was not the ideas, nor her ability to communicate them which was the root cause of the problem. There was, she found, a link to active listening, the conscious effort that is required, in order to listen for the purposes of understanding, rather than just hearing what someone has to say. She examined what was actually involved in effective communication, in active listening and the circumstances which may prevent it. In doing so, she found there was a connection to the perceived level of authority assigned to the people involved in the exchange. Upon deeper exploration, she also found there was a connection to an invisible set of rules which appeared to govern how such a level of authority was granted, who it was granted by and to whom, the naming conventions for which were interchangeable, depending on the situation.

Under the arbitrary banners of custom, tradition, social convention, political opinion, popular opinion, public opinion, social expectation, common good or god's will, the rules seemed to say that no matter what she did, her mind, her thoughts, ideas, her body, her life, were not her own, that she had no level of ruling authority over her own life, and the standard by which she would be judged was not her own. If she failed at something, it was either 'the will of god' or 'she brought it on herself'. If she succeeded, it was either 'the love of god,' or 'who does she think she is'. The measures of what was deemed to be a successful, productive, happy life were not her own to define; the measures were defined for her and required subservience, duty and giving without question or condition. Her ability to think, to feel, to give and receive love, to pursue enjoyment and her own happiness was not her own and came with multiple caveats and impossible conditions: contradictions could and should be ignored; there was no need for reason or logic, or to even think or talk about such things, others could and would do that thinking and talking for her. The impossible conditions included the commonly held belief that, before her life even began, she was deemed evil, a sinner, and would remain so until the day she died, then upon her death she would face the judgement of a god, when she would be either rewarded, or punished for the contradictions she had ignored; for the paths she had or had not followed; for the choices she had or had not made in her life.

Deriving any enjoyment from life was, it seemed, punishable by both life and death; the punishment was for others, a higher level of authority, particularly god, to decide and judge her for, her own judgement, her own ability to question and decide what was right and wrong, null, void, and irrelevant. All that was ever needed was, to merely exist for the sake of others, to only listen to those in authority but not question anything, to raise children and heirs, pay taxes, contribute to society, silently follow the status quo, to produce another generation, who would repeat the cycle. The conclusion she arrived at was that, if there was little or nothing to enjoy about life or living, and that even beyond death, there was no guarantee of enjoying that either, then life could not have any meaning at all, for anyone and was pointless.

This entire way of thinking which she was apparently expected to follow was, to her young mind, incredulous and there was nothing she found good about it. It spoke nothing of actual reality, of love, laughter, fun, play, tenderness, understanding, or beauty, which as far as she was concerned, she had every right to feel towards herself first, before anyone else. It spoke nothing of the truly inspirational people who across the ages, had learned how to grow crops; to raise animals; discovered fire; had built ships; used navigation to cross oceans and explore new lands; the producers: farmers, cooks, doctors, inventors, engineers, builders, scientists - the iconic people from all walks of life who had by the product of their own work, progressed and made the world a better place, actual reality, even better.

Why anyone could be convinced that there was an even better world, heaven, or a worse one, hell, waiting after death, confounded her because it seemed to void the current world, the real and tangible one. She could see, hear, touch, feel, the world around her. The reality of living in it, in the faces and expressions of people, her parents, grandparents, children, family, friends, in birdsong, rainfall, mountains, rivers, oceans, the sky, in art, literature, music, food, flowers and trees. She saw beauty in the wondrous, magnificent world around her, why anyone could or should be punished, or made to feel guilty or ashamed for enjoying it and seeing the world as beautiful, confounded her even more.

Charlie often wondered about the phrase 'rose tinted glasses' and why it was used as a way of making another human feel bad for viewing the world positively. She was not ignorant of pain, illness, loss, grief, fear, hatred, sadness, anger, and violence; she was not immune to those aspects of life; she had experienced all of them, many times, but rather than being entirely consumed by that which was ugly, bad, or malevolent, those aspects seemed to accentuate the beautiful reality of the world around her even more.

Charlie plotted the many pathways she saw ahead for her life and examined the choices each pathway presented: accept the impossible, conflicted rules, the code set by others for her; or forge her own code, for her own life. She tried, at first, as best she could to accept the impossible rules, but doing so nearly destroyed her; the remnants of the attempt had taken many years to remove. She concluded that by removing ideas of a god, then ruling out the existence of an afterlife, and then making her very own self responsible and accountable for herself and her actions, she found that what remained was life, her life. Free of the ties of a life involving punishment in one form or another, she saw the freedom available to her, to live her life wholly and truly, entirely, and solely responsible for her own choices, for the consequences of her actions or choices, and the subsequent actions associated with those consequences. She knew, even then, that she would encounter struggle, she would face hurt and be hurt because she knew others would not understand nor want to. There were many things that she knew would take time for her to understand, but she prepared and then she went to work on living.

Charlie, at the age of fifteen, by taking a part time job, discovered that she loved working. The days were often long, tiring and stressful but that had little significance to her. She was a fast learner. She found that understanding what needed to be done, and then finding better, more efficient, less expensive ways of achieving the same task, came naturally to her. She embraced what she was doing, the thinking about what she was doing, and above all, she simply loved doing.

Going back to school, she spoke to her friends about her job, but they did not seem to share her excitement of working and wanting to do more of it. By then, Charlie could not wait to finish school. She knew there was much that she had yet to learn, but that learning what needed to be learned solely from the confines of a classroom no longer appealed to her. The mode of learning which taught and required her to blindly accept and follow what she was told, to just memorise and repeat rather than to understand and listen to understand, had no appeal to her.

She was often described as a difficult student, a loner, incapable of fitting in, who would never amount to anything. To a teenage girl, though these words were hurtful as they were spoken, she found they had no meaning to her because there was no information given as to what 'difficult', or 'fitting in', or 'anything', meant.

She continued with multiple part time jobs, and again found that no matter the job, she loved working. The skills and experience she had acquired in the previous jobs carried over into the next. The money she earned was important, but it was not her primary motivation; learning and acquiring knowledge that would update, or could be appended to, her existing knowledge for reapplying elsewhere was.

Though a vision of what type of business she would have or where escaped her, she knew that someday, she would build and run her own company. She saw her goal, and the many blanks, the unknowns in her knowledge of how to achieve her objective, but she knew that with time, she would fill those blanks, each and every one of them.

When she graduated school, she continued her part-time work, but to get some form of qualification, Charlie opted for a local college because it ran courses specifically designed to meet the needs of a large local employer. That the local company invested heavily, to put a means of sourcing and equipping a talent pool right on their own doorstep, resonated with her. The subjects she studied she enjoyed, because they fit with her natural enjoyment of working, of thinking, of discovery, of enterprise, of innovation, productivity and finding new ways of doing things.

Each time that Charlie now stepped into the training rooms of Endeavour, she was reminded of the very first day that she had joined that large company from college and had set foot in theirs. That job was formative to Charlie as she had observed everything from how the company was set up and run, and by whom, to the interpersonal relationships between her, her colleagues and managers, the role of managers, what they did, how they did it, the role of different departments and department leaders, the role of the employees, how they were trained, how performance was measured, what was expected of them, for how long, and if individual talent, skill and thinking outside the box, was punished, or rewarded.

She discovered how successes were celebrated or dismissed as unimportant. She saw who was held responsible and accountable for problems and issues, who was called to fix them, how the problems affected morale, relationships with clients, and external reputation.

She noted an often-large gulf between the business leaders, managers, and different levels of employees. The chasm, it seemed to Charlie, was not necessarily caused by views held about rank, superiority or authority but by a fundamental lack of knowledge, understanding, recognition or appreciation of the individual value, the purpose, the role or responsibilities of the other. Managers were brought in to manage and supervise, without ever having to know who, or what exactly, it was they were managing. Staff were recruited often in large numbers, and with minimal or no training were expected to follow a vague set of processes, procedures or read from a script, without ever being given any context about the function or purpose of that which they were expected to follow.

There was an expectation that everyone should automatically know, without it ever being confirmed that they did. In the early days, why they did not say 'I don't know' and set out to learn and find out, puzzled her.

Despite the political and often delicate social interactions which she observed, Charlie also loved that job, and she progressed and thrived in it. Instead of waiting for change to happen around or for her, she enacted changes herself. A year into it, Charlie was promoted to a role as trainer, where she promptly discarded the previous programme, replacing it with one of her own design, built around the individuals she would be training, their roles, and the customers they would be interacting with.

It was in this role that Charlie glimpsed another way of running a business, which as far as she could see, had never been tried, or at scale. Assessing aspects of the idea carefully, she realised it was not impossible, it was very possible, and very lucrative.

She understood that she still needed time to get more experience, more information, and more resources, so she put herself through university to get her master's degree in economics, supporting herself as she did so with part time jobs. Whatever obstacles she encountered she overcame because her sole objective was to learn, and discover as much as she could, always working towards her goal.

When she had earned her degree, she furnished herself with more experience, achieved by working across industry sectors, countries, companies, and roles. Though each company was different in terms of type, function, size and shape, there was little evident difference in how they were being run and operated. There was a common theme she found, which related back to knowledge and the use of it, which was that companies were asking, indeed expecting, that customers would tell them what to do, without first knowing or understanding what their own value to that customer was, where it came from or how to describe it.

When there was nothing more for Charlie to learn or discover by working for someone else, she set up her own business, Value Signals Consulting. Her proposition was simple: guide her clients towards understanding their own value by examining their entire business, by working in it, as if she were part of it, as a means of understanding each part of it. Her services were expensive but her reputation for getting the work done faster, with expert efficiency and to greater outcomes and results, preceded her. She had no difficulty whatsoever finding clients; they sought her out. She had grown her business rapidly and within the second year, it had turned over half a million dollars in after tax profit. Eventually, she had moved herself and her business to London, and then she had transferred the business, along with herself, to the United States, and had retained all of her clients, under Endeavour.

Following an unusual chain of events which Michael had initiated, it had taken two months for her and the team to form Endeavour; by month three it had started trading; within nine months they had rapidly outgrown the temporary premises they had rented. With a steady stream of income generated by a growing number of customers and clients, in the first year, Endeavour had returned over a half million dollars' worth of profit and had steadily grown in the years since. Now here she was – five years after Endeavour headquarters had been built and had opened its doors, proudly casting her eyes over the new group of twelve people in front of her, men and women of all ages, backgrounds, roles and positions, anticipation on their faces – the chief of Endeavour.

In her opening statement to the group, she said, "It is possible to extend the runway only so many times, but eventually, in order to fly, one has to leave the ground and take off. If flying is the goal, taking off is the only way of achieving it. Taking off is the accomplishment, flying is the reward. The core purpose of Endeavour, for all the customers we do business with, and indeed each of you here, lies in the taking off and making it as easy as possible for them, and you, to do so. We do not work for our customers, nor do they for us. You do not work for me; I do not work for you. You work together but you do not work for each other. Our customers work for their own benefit and profit. I work for my own, you for yours. I can help and support you, yes, but I cannot do your work for you, we cannot do all the work for our customers. We do not work on the basis of force, coercion, or duress. We work on the basis of agreement. That agreement is achieved through a mutual understanding of what the other is working towards, and why. Endeavour provides the runway, the tools, the conditions needed for, and maintaining flight, to then reach the intended destination. Taking off, then maintaining the conditions needed for the flight, can only be achieved by doing. I am responsible for Endeavour in its entirety, but the responsibility for taking off is not mine or Endeavour's, it is your own, that is your own value to discover."

Over the course of many hours, she continued to facilitate the group's journey into Endeavour, and introduced them to the Endeavour framework of working. It was up to each of them, with guidance and support from Charlie and her team, to take that framework and make it their own. She studied each individual in the group, in respect to their interactions, their questions, and responses, storing and updating notes in her mind. Sending them on their way, she wondered if all of the twelve would return to Endeavour the following day; she hoped they would, but hope was not a guarantee.

When she reached her office, taking in the expanse of the

San Diego city skyline, and the bay horizon off in the distance, she was met with the sight and fragrance of a beautiful arrangement of chrysanthemums positioned on her desk. She reached for the envelope nestled in the middle, recognising the penmanship of David Banner, one of her dearest friends, and Endeavour's chief of Talent Value and Learning.

Stepping away from her desk, and closer to the glass, she smiled and read the message inside: 'Happy birthday, Charlie. We love you, and we are proud of you. Signed with our love, from all at Endeavour'. The joyous smile on her face broadened, as she looked down towards the Endeavour Enterprise and Trade Centre, next to which stood the jewel in the company's crown, the Endeavour Training Academy, two low rise buildings, both open to the public, teeming with people, and those people were her customers, and the customers of her customers.

She sat down at her desk and with a fingerprint touch signed into her computer. The company wide message board was full of birthday messages to which she responded simply with, 'Thank you, the flowers are beautiful. I love and I am proud of you all too.'

Shifting her focus from her birthday back to business, she began to read the centrally available daily updates from across the business which awaited her review. She started with the summary report from Jane Adams, the wife of David Banner, and the head of Technology and Cyber Operations, a genius, and close friend whom she admired and loved dearly. Scanning it, she noted the reference to an unusual, increasing spike in online activity referring to the company and to Charlie herself. Louisa, chief of marketing and communications, referenced the spike too but indicated that they had not made any changes to their marketing strategy or campaigns.

She moved on to the other summaries, noting that Devon Forsyth, head of Legal, and Samuel Walker, head of Endeavour Treasury both made references to an increase in website searches for financial reports and freedom of information requests, though neither of which applied to Endeavour.

As she continued reading, making notes and comments in the files, she saw a message arrive from Jane which said, 'There is more noise, we have identified the originating source location, and are attempting to separate the signal from the noise, David, Devon, Amy, Louisa, Andrea, Sam and I, and Sai of course are monitoring the situation and will stay on top of it. See you in the morning. Love to you and Michael.'

She replied, 'Thank you, Jane. See you tomorrow. Charlie.'

To her phone she voiced a message to Michael saying, 'Leaving Endeavour in ten, my love. Is she ready?'

His reply chirped back and read, 'She is. See you soon, my darling.'

CHAPTER THREE - BLINDED BY THE SIGHT

Shawn Trammel was bored as he sat in the audience of the education-blah-something-blah-conference in Sacramento which Edward Prestbury had begged him to show up to.

Edward had claimed there would be several powerful people at the conference from all over the state, including the governor, and if Shawn wanted to get elected to congress, he would need to be seen as supportive of schools, colleges and universities and their plight, because he would need their vote, and the support of lobby groups.

Shawn was, he thought to himself, already a powerful man. He came from a wealthy family and had inherited a small fortune. He had never wanted to work a day in his life, and was shrewd enough to know that if he did not want to work, he would need to look after his money, so he invested most of his fortune and relied on his investment bank to do the work for him.

He was a shrewd, conniving and cunning man who enjoyed finding ways of getting others to do the work for him. Aged nineteen, he had gone to an Ivy League school, and had picked accounting as a field of study because it would require the least amount of work or effort on his part, and there would always be a student who would be willing to take money from him, and do his assignments for him. Edward Prestbury was one of them. Harry Downes was another but at least Harry was just as shrewd and conniving as Shawn and they, together with a band of cohorts who they had met in college and over the decades since, had enjoyed plenty of what they called fun, usually at the expense of others, and had become far wealthier in the process.

Shawn had no real interest in politics or actually being a congressman; he had taken the challenge on as a bet, and so far, there was little for him to do, except show up to events here and there, wine and dine some influential people, take their money for his campaign, make lots of promises, use lots of charm and ties to his family and his wealth.

He enjoyed seeing people squirm, so when the journalist attending the conference stood up, introduced himself and then began to ask questions to Edward about a company called Endeavour, the boredom Shawn had felt suddenly evaporated. He saw Edward's face redden with temper and embarrassment as the murmurs from the audience grew louder. Shawn spotted an opportunity, not to help Edward out of his plight, but to use the scenario playing out in front of him to his advantage in order to get the fame, the support, and the vote of the bodies in the audience as a way of getting to Congress.

Thinking quickly, he stood up and said out loud, so the whole room could hear him, "Mr Sewell, is it? I am Mr Shawn Trammel, and I believe Mr Prestbury up there said he has no comment, because he and I have an extensive plan in motion, on how to protect our wonderful institutes of education, all across this country from the threat of large, greedy, profit hungry companies and unfair competition. It is great and vital to see competition thriving between our colleges and universities but outside competition from a company like Endeavour, which directly threatens the jobs of people who work in our schools, is not welcome. Mr Prestbury and I were planning to speak to the governor about the plan today, but the governor seems to be absent from this conference, which is a surprise as I thought education was important to him. I would welcome the opportunity to speak to you, Mr Sewell, or anyone here who takes education seriously and agrees that our system of education needs to be protected."

Shawn was irritated by the slightly delayed reaction to his statement from the audience, but soon there was a rapturous applause, which made him forget his irritation as he thought getting to Congress would be easier than he had imagined, and he would win the bet. He was also delighted to see that Edward's expression showed confusion mixed with fury.

Afterwards when the conference segment discussion had ended, Edward found himself struggling to break through the crowd of people surrounding Shawn. When he eventually resorted to almost bulldozing his way through, he pulled Shawn to one side and with a desperate tone of plea in his voice asked, "What plan, Shawn?"

"Edward, don't be a fool, you know as well as I do that there is no plan, but I am sure, given how important you said my being at this conference was to you, and to my getting to Congress, that you will find a plan, won't you? Unfortunately, I cannot help you with that, as I need to leave now, as I have other more important places to be, one of which is very likely to be a meeting with the governor who won't be too happy about what I just said, but he will easily forget."

CHAPTER FOUR - HINDSIGHT

Stepping out into the warm afternoon sunshine once again made Charlie smile, as she took in the San Diego downtown skyline which she loved so dearly. They had purchased the expansive plot of land, on which the three Endeavour buildings now stood, shortly after the company had started trading, when the business had rapidly outgrown the temporary rented premises which they had used as a sandbox to test operational and financial aspects of the Endeavour business plan.

Robyn Foster, her brother Anthony, and his construction team had worked quickly to develop and complete construction of all three buildings over the course of a year. Each building was in its own way, a symbol of pride to Charlie, but her favourite was Endeavour headquarters, the soaring, sheer height of it, the steel erection starting many floors underground, which then jutted to the sky, encased in reflective glass which acted both as a mirror and a source of power, the beautiful tensile strength of its structure and form, hidden from the outside.

She switched on the engine of her Tesla Model S, and began her drive home, revelling in the brilliant product of intelligent technology and automotive engineering at her disposal. Every time she sat into her car, or any car, or observed any form of machinery, be that spacecraft, trains, aircraft, medical devices, robotics, or technology, she delighted in the fact that every time she did so, she was celebrating human innovation. She was celebrating the person, the team of people, who would very likely never be known to her, but who had made the impossible possible, and the proof of it was real, tangible, she was driving just one example of that proof. Her own company was another proof, Sai was yet another and she was immensely proud.

Empowered by the thought, she enjoyed the silence of the drive, the scent of the flowers brought her mind to her birthday, and from there to her age. Age and time are funny concepts, she thought. She understood why women and men, in equal measure, she had found, were often driven by a fear of running out of time. For many people, wanting to have children and raising a family was an important step in their lives, but to Charlie such a step was not a goal for her, nor for Michael. As she thought of her family, of Michael and in particular that which was Endeavour, she adored her extended and expanding family.

As far as she was concerned, her age did not define her, and life happened no matter what her age was. When she met Michael, it was neither planned or organised, it just happened. She had, of course, learned the hard way to stop herself from associating goals and achievements with her age. The most memorable being when she reached twenty, she had set a deadline for herself which was that by age twenty-three, she would have her own business. When the day of her twenty-third birthday came around, she had not achieved her own deadline and felt disappointed and discouraged as a result. It had taken time for her to adjust her thinking, and to stop placing her own barriers in front of herself, barriers which served no purpose, other than as self-imposed measures of failure. She laughed to herself when she considered that by age twenty-six, she had her own consulting firm, running precisely the type of business she had always worked towards and wanted.

She learned that 'can' presupposes 'want', and both have to be in agreement. If presented with a locked box that she wanted to open, but the key for it she could not find, then the box, no matter how much she may want it, could not be opened, unless by the use of force, which then ran the risk of destroying the box and that which lay within. She smiled to herself now when she considered how the key to the box was in front of her all along back then but hidden under the debris of being more concerned by her age than what she was doing and achieving.

As she pulled up to the gates of the beautiful La Jolla home she shared with Michael, she thought back to the day she had turned eighteen while living and working in Paris. She could not recall many of her birthdays after that, with two beautiful, magnificent exceptions. The first was the very best of birthdays, the precise moment of which she had first met the man now standing in front of her, at the door to their home. The second was the birthday when he had proudly stood in front of her and their friends and had asked her to marry him.

CHAPTER FIVE - FIRST SIGHT

Michael Weston, while waiting for the elevator to arrive on the floor of the London hotel he was staying in, stood gazing at a sculpture positioned on a small antique mahogany table, between the bank of lifts. Dressed casually, he was going to have breakfast in the hotel and then check on final preparations for the international banking conference, which he, as president of Capital Enterprise Bank, would be opening later on that morning.

"I wonder how many people see that beautiful piece of sculpture, but do not notice or consider it?"

The sound of the woman's voice, which had spoken so suddenly from behind his back, made him jump. In the instant it had taken for him to hear the words, Michael could not decide which startled him more, the beautiful voice that had said them, or that she had stated with precision, what it was that he had just been thinking.

As he pivoted around to follow the voice, his eyes fell on the most beautiful woman he had ever seen, slender yet curvaceous, formally attired in a tailored dress suit, with an elegant, yet commanding poise, and a face and neck which begged to be touched and kissed as lightly as a feather. Her eyes, he thought, he had painted for most of his life, so he knew colours intimately, yet he had never known that such a shade of blue existed anywhere, eyes so full of life, intelligent, piercing, which were now fixed, intently, on him.

"You are either a witch or a mind-reader. I was thinking precisely that."

Smiling, her eyes still fixed on him, she said, "I can assure you that I am neither. I apologise for startling you."

"That you did, but I do not know which was more surprising, the voice suddenly speaking behind me, or that you said exactly what I was thinking," he said, then queried, "Who are you, and where did you come from?"

"I am Charlie Rochford. I am a hotel guest; my room is just down the hall and I imagine it was likely both." Charlie answered with ease, taking in everything about the man in front of her.

He smiled and he said, "You are right, Charlie, it was both, and I am Michael Weston."

She smiled, held out her hand to shake his, and as he responded in kind, she said, "Good morning, Michael."

"Good morning to you too, Charlie."

Charlie was quite sure that she was staring at him, just as intently as Michael seemed to be gazing at her. His tall, broad, and strong body, his quietly confident stature, his easy smile, eyes that were alert, aware, taking in everything about her as she was of him, and his deep voice, such a beautiful voice, flecked with the tones of both British and American accents. *The way he said my name*, she thought, she had never heard it said that way before. She wanted to hear him say it again. She silently considered if he was perhaps an artist, there was something about the way in which he was gazing at her, the way his eyes moved, as if he was painting an image in his mind; she decided that it was a strong possibility and very much looked forward to finding out if she was right.

Michael was thinking to himself, as he watched her, about an image he would paint and he decided that it would be of her eyes; he was enchanted and mesmerised by them, by her, all of her.

He watched her suddenly step forward and press the button for the elevator, then she grinned brightly at him and said, "If you want to go anywhere in a lift, Michael, it usually helps to press the button. That magnificent sculpture there is beautiful, but it cannot press the button for you; it has little arms which are far too short to reach."

Michael laughed and with a smile that seemed to stretch ear to ear, and replied, "Of all the mornings, in all the world, of all the lifts I have ever waited for in all of my life, I never thought the day would come, Charlie, when I would find myself overjoyed by the fact that I had forgotten to press the button."

The sound of his laughter, the way and ease with which he said her name again were a symphony to her ears.

As the elevator pinged its arrival and they stepped in, his arm guarding and guiding her, Charlie said, "I am delighted too, Michael." As she said it, the smile on his face and in his eyes matched hers.

On their way down in the elevator to the lobby, though they had only just met, they found themselves chatting as if they were two old friends.

Michael learned that it was her birthday, that Charlie lived in Dublin, Ireland and was in London for the week with a new client of her own firm.

She told him why she thought he was an artist. Astonished by her perceptiveness, he confirmed that though he worked as the president of an American bank, his passion was, and always had been, painting and art. He told her about the conference, about the opening speech he would be delivering that morning.

Making their way from the lifts towards the dining room, signing in at the door, they saw it was full, with only one table left tucked away in the corner. They took it, both ordered coffee and omelettes, and continued talking.

He talked about his parents, his father an electrical engineer and his mother, a physicist, both originally from Colchester, England, who had emigrated to the United States with his two older siblings when he was ten years old, and created a new life for themselves in Pasadena, California. He told her that he had just finalised his second divorce, the timing of his trip to London being a welcome relief to mark the end of the proceedings, a new beginning in many ways.

She listened intently to everything he said and when their coffee arrived, he suggested they clink cups to celebrate her birthday, to which she blushed and laughed, and then they did.

As their food arrived, Charlie talked about her life in Dublin, her parents, her siblings and large Irish family, and the relationship which she had recently ended. She told him about her consulting business, her plans to move to London as a means of expanding her business. She also told him that she could not remember the last time that she had enjoyed a breakfast so much, to which he wholeheartedly agreed.

Michael watched Charlie as they talked, her eyes sparkling, as she spoke so animatedly, about her life, and he, for the first time in his life, had found himself describing his, so freely and easily, had wondered how to find a way to meet and see her again.

He had cycled through every possible reason why he should not want to meet her again: he had only just met her; she was younger than he; his divorce; they lived in different countries; he had his job to focus on; he would only be in London for a week; that the way he felt about a woman he had only just met was impossible. Examining what he thought, at first, to be all valid reasons, he soon realised they were not reasons, they were excuses. Michael, renowned for his skill at making seemingly impossible situations possible, now found himself in what he could only describe as a helpless and hopeless one.

As they finished breakfast, and began to walk out of the dining room, it seemed to occur to both of them, at the same time, that they would be parting soon. Charlie, noting a flicker of sadness on Michael's face, which she also felt, reached into her handbag, extracted a business card, handed it to him, and said, "In the event that you, over the course of today, wonder if your meeting me this morning was a figment of your imagination, here is my card."

With a nervous quality to her voice, she added, "I will be finished work at five o'clock this evening. The office is right across the street so I will be back here soon after that. I am staying in room six-one-zero-six. When you are done with your conference, if you have no plans afterwards, give me a call, and perhaps we can make some?"

Michael, in complete astonishment at the recognition that the situation was neither helpless nor hopeless, said, "As serendipity would have it, I am in room six-one-zero-eight." As he took the card from her hand, he smiled, then gently took her hand and said, "I will see you this evening, Charlie."

Smiling back at him, she turned to walk away from him, and said, "You will, and until then, I hope that you enjoy a wonderful day."

Holding her card in his hand, he followed the sight of her as she walked out of the hotel. When he could no longer see her, and with her last words ringing in his ears, he set off for the conference room. Satisfied to see that preparations had been completed; he went back to his room to change into his suit. As he did so, he thought about how, when he had woken that morning, he had felt anxious about the conference, whereas now, his apprehension had vanished. He would see her again this evening, which was, he thought, the best reward he could ever possibly have anticipated.

Charlie walked to the office of her new client, feeling as light as a feather as she did so. Signing in at the front desk, then making her way upstairs to meet her client, she felt a swell of happiness and pride rising within herself. She thought of when she had seen him standing by the elevator, deep in contemplation, focused on the sculpture, the way he startled as she spoke, and then as he turned to look at her, the eyes that met hers, were in some inexplicable way, familiar. It took much strength for her to focus on the day ahead and contain her excitement at the thought of seeing Michael again that evening. By the time she reached her client, she had focused and settled in to begin her workday, thinking that she enjoyed her job on any given day, no matter how stressful or difficult the day could be, but today, she anticipated she would enjoy it all the more.

Charlie and Michael thought of one another many times over the course of their day. Michael had put her card in his pocket, and every once in a while, took it out to look at it, astounded at how accurate her statement was that without it, he may well have thought her a figment of his imagination. Charlie thought of Michael whenever she saw someone with a coffee cup, smiling as she remembered his clinking hers to celebrate her birthday.

Later, as she was leaving the office of her client and heading back to the hotel, she wondered if he would be waiting for her. Though she had no reason to believe that he would be, she found herself in hopeful anticipation of it. Entering the hotel, she scanned the lobby for him, but he was nowhere to be seen. She stepped into the waiting elevator, she pressed the button for her floor, and in the journey up dismissed the nudge of disappointment she felt. When the elevator doors opened on her floor and she stepped out, to her delight and amazement, she saw him casually leaning on the table on which the sculpture stood.

"Michael, do you enjoy waiting around elevators as a hobby, or were you waiting for me?"

"Elevators are not a hobby of mine, so yes, I was waiting for you."

"How long have you been waiting?"

"It does not matter how long, Charlie, you are here now."

"Why were you waiting for me, Michael?"

"Well, firstly I wanted to surprise you which from the look on your face, I achieved precisely that, and secondly, rather than call you, I would much rather see you."

"You did. I am delighted by it, Michael, and I would much rather see you too."

Walking at a leisurely pace down the long corridor towards their rooms, which they had discovered that morning were side by side, they chatted about their respective days. Michael told her about the adrenaline rush which he had felt upon completing his opening address at the conference. He admitted that he had looked at her business card many times over the day.

Charlie smiled and admitted how every coffee cup she had seen that day reminded her of him.

When they discussed what to do for the evening, without any hesitation or disagreement, they opted for a stroll across the River Thames. Giving themselves fifteen minutes to get changed, Charlie told him to knock on her door when he was ready to go.

She laughed when less than ten minutes later she heard a tap on her door, opening it to find Michael showered and changed into a beautiful teal coloured shirt and dark navy jeans.

He laughed too when he saw that she had showered and changed her clothes, her hair tumbling down her shoulders, and was, as she opened the door, hopping on one leg, struggling to put on a boot.

He said, "I have never known a woman to get ready so fast."

Smiling, in acknowledgement, she said, "There are many things you do not know about me yet. That I am not like any other woman is one of them."

Without any hesitation whatsoever, he replied, "Oh, my dearest, Charlie, it is true that there are many things I do not know about you yet, but that you are not like any other woman is one of the very first things I understood about you."

"You are not like any other man I have ever met either, Michael."

She fixed her boot, grabbed her jacket, door key and handbag, and they went on their way to spend their first evening together, talking as they walked in the late June evening sunshine of London. She told him that her house in Dublin had sold, so her move to London had been initiated, and her legal team were handling the paperwork for the relocation of her business to London. *It is amazing,* Charlie thought, as she walked beside him, *how easy, and comfortable it is to talk to him, as if I can say anything to him and I want to tell him everything.*

When she told him so, he stopped in his tracks, a tender look of sheer amazement on his face, and said, "Charlie, I do not know how you do it, but I was just thinking the same thing about you. It is truly a rare occasion for me, to suddenly find something that I didn't even know I was missing."

"It is a rarity for me too, Michael."

Crossing over Monument bridge, they giggled and laughed at the sight of two swans who Charlie had decided were in the middle of an argument. He erupted into peals of laughter as she filled him in on what she thought they were arguing about. He was truly enthralled by her ability to make him feel relaxed, at ease and just himself. They found a restaurant along the bank which was busy but not full and in no time, they were seated at a table by the window, and had resumed their conversation. They shared more about themselves: their lives, their families, about their work, he talked about his childhood, their move from England to the United States, his previous marriages, why he chose and persisted with a career at the bank as a means of supporting his painting. She talked about her business, why she loved working, and even more so now that she worked for herself.

When he spoke, she listened to every word, absorbing everything about him, and found herself captivated by him. Michael listened intently to every word Charlie said, speaking so candidly about herself, and her life. He was mesmerised by the sight of her blue eyes sparkling, every expression and gesture radiating, it seemed to him, with pure love and light. As she explained her outlook on life, about the method which she used for living, she saw the look of complete astonishment on his face, as if with every word she was saying she was handing him a precious gemstone. Concerned for him, she gently asked, "Michael, are you okay?"

He took a deep breath in and gathered his thoughts.

"I can assure you, Charlie, that I am more than okay. Indeed, listening to what you just said, I have never, in all the years I have lived on this Earth, felt as good as I do, right here and now, with you. As I already told you, though I work in banking, I am, have always been, and will always be an artist. For years, I have considered at length why I adore and enjoy painting so much, and why it is that no matter what happens in my work, my passion for painting is what drives me. I have never believed in the existence of a god, or that my ability to paint, to create a piece of art, is a consequence of some miracle of design on the part of another.

"Those who have seen my work often ask how it is that I can take a blank canvas, a brush, a selection of colours and create something so beautiful, from nothing. The question has perplexed me, because I am not creating something from nothing. I am painting from a supply of images, visual ideas if you will, which I have captured and stored in my mind. Those images are perceived from that which I can see, hear, touch, feel, and the reality of this world in which I live. The part which has perplexed me all the more, is the description of my work as beautiful, when all that I see, around me, in this, the real world, is beautiful. I have never fully grasped Charlie, until now, why it is that I see the world as beautiful, yet others do not. I have lived and at many times survived because of my passion for picking up a paintbrush and with delicate, sometimes violent strokes of paint, creating a piece that brings my sense of life to life. That passion, fuelling my insistence that though there is bad, pain and sadness in the world, which I am not blind to, I have painted them too, that I do not care to see only those aspects, nor be consumed by them. For years, Charlie, I have longed for, and struggled to find, anyone who could even come close to understanding the entirety of what it is that I mean, yet here you, Charlie Rochford, are, not only understanding it, but you have also articulated it so precisely."

Charlie's eyes shone with tears as she heard the deep unspoken truth of his statement, which echoed deep within her. She moved her hand gently to his, placed hers over his and said tenderly, "You are not alone, Michael. There are two of us now. I have felt that too."

For an instant, in an effort to hide the tears that had formed in his eyes from her, all he could do was stare at her beautiful hand covering his. Just as quickly he realised that he had nothing to hide from her, and that above all, he did not want to hide anything from her. In response to her hand on this, he curled his fingers around hers, lifted his eyes to meet hers, and said simply, "There are two of us now."

It seemed to Charlie, when she felt his fingers curl around hers, saw the tears in his eyes as she heard him speak, that the rest of the world had disappeared around her leaving just the two of them.

"Is it just me, Charlie, or has the rest of the world disappeared?"

"Yes, it has for me too," she smiled in reply.

For the rest of their evening in the restaurant, they celebrated life and their meeting each other so unexpectedly, they celebrated her birthday, and enjoyed delicious food. They laughed a lot; they shared themselves, their thoughts, and often comfortable silences as they dined together. She erupted with laughter when Michael, teasing her with his natural good humour, had asked if startling a man examining sculpture by elevators was a hobby for her. He chuckled when she had said that it was a hobby, and a very enjoyable one.

On leaving the restaurant, she curled her hand around his, he intertwined his fingers with hers, and they walked back over the bridge towards the hotel, hand in hand, no thought of past or future, only their mutual enjoyment of the present, and each other.

Reaching the door of her hotel room, she said, "Goodnight, Michael. I will see you in the morning."

He leaned in, kissed her softly on her cheek, and replied quietly, "Goodnight, Charlie, and that you will."

As Charlie and Michael went to sleep in their own beds that night, though separated, they both felt each other's presence, a closeness to the other. Both slept soundly, the memory of that day, and anticipation of a new one filling their dreams.

Her first thought when she woke at the crack of dawn, was naturally of Michael. He had told her that, like her, he was an early riser, so she picked up the phone, called to order coffee and breakfast for two to be delivered to his room, charged to hers with instructions to knock on her door when it was delivered.

When the hotel porter arrived with breakfast ten minutes later, she wrapped herself in the fluffy hotel bathrobe, went to Michael's door, giggling as she heard the puzzled sound of his voice saying that he had not ordered anything. As he opened the door and saw her standing there, the look of surprise and blissful delight on his face was a sight she hoped she would be able to see for the rest of her life.

Michael, getting over his initial surprise, realised that seeing her there was most unexpected, yet the most natural thing in the world.

He grinned at her and said, "Good morning, Charlie."

"Good morning to you, Michael."

As Charlie signed for the breakfast, then wheeled the breakfast trolley into his room, he asked huskily, "And where, Charlie, are we having breakfast?"

Charlie, amused and thrilled at the tone of this voice, pointed towards his bed and answered, "There."

Michael watched her, aware of her entire presence, of every motion she made, thinking about how, when he had woken in the middle of the night, his first thought was of her, wishing and wanting her, by his side, in his bed. Now that she was here, he could not decide what he wanted.

Charlie perceptively sensed, as she saw him watching her, that his thoughts were a blend between indecision and desire. To give him time to adjust to her suddenly being in his room, she picked up the pot of coffee and two cups and set them down on his bedside table. She stepped to him, reached her hand to his face, then standing on tiptoes, she kissed him softly on his lips. With an impish smile on her face, she stepped back from him, walked to the other side of the bed, and climbed in under the soft duvet.

Michael smiled and laughed, when he saw her, with an easy, natural motion, pat his side of the bed, in a gesture for him to join her. As the new day dawned through the window of his London hotel room, Michael and Charlie spent the early morning together, side by side in bed, sipping coffee, both reverently watching the sun rise, while talking as comfortably as they had the day before.

Later that evening, when they had both finished work, anticipating that he would be there, Charlie had found him, waiting for her by the elevator and was thrilled that he was. Without saying a word as his eyes met hers, Michael gently pulled her toward his tall, lean body. Cupping her beautiful chin with his hands, he leaned down and kissed her fervently, which she returned with a passion matching his.

Though saying anything was not quite necessary, it occurred to Charlie that somehow, they would need to make it down the corridor. Smiling at him, as she broke away from him, she said, "Michael, I hope you do not kiss every woman you see getting off an elevator like that."

Michael laughed, clasped her hand in his, and said, "When that woman is you, then I will."

With the pull of desire pulsing in their veins, they raced each other down the corridor. By the time they had reached her room, stepped through the door, letting it close behind them, there was no force in the universe strong enough to separate them. Clothes dropped to the floor in a line that ran towards the bed. Naked when they reached it, his strong arms holding her as she fell on the bed, he felt her slender legs around his waist as he followed her. The feel of her skin, his body on hers, the sound of her arousal heightened his. Her eyes radiant with desire, fixed on him, she pulled him even closer with her hips, then she felt him, deep within her. To the searingly intense rhythm of her body beneath his, he watched her, and he felt her, the fury of her desire rising with his, her back arching upwards, closer to his body, taking him even deeper still, the release in perfect unison, as he felt the powerful clutch of her muscles, to the pulsation of his. Tenderly, he kissed her as she basked in the weight of this body on hers, the feeling of his damp skin underneath her fingertips. Neither wanting to move, they lay there, both exploring each other, and delighting in the pleasure of doing so.

When they eventually moved, they talked about what to do for the evening, and for the remainder of the week. They wondered if they had both gone crazy, but as they talked it through, they agreed that they were not. Neither were led to act purely upon emotion and the situation they found themselves in now, together, and delighting in being so, was not something either of them had taken lightly, both wanting to explore it further and do so together. They agreed that spending as much time together as they could was at the top of the list, and that it would be more easily achieved by him checking out of his room and moving in with her.

Michael chuckled in agreement when Charlie told him that the reason for proposing he move in with her was, though he had far less luggage than she, he was messier than her. As neither saw any reason to wait, they wasted no time, and rearranged their accommodation with the hotel, and having done so, they spent every morning, evening, and night together.

In their time together, Michael sketched many pictures of her. He went with her to see properties in London which she had shortlisted to purchase. He brought Charlie to see the house and neighbourhood where he had spent the first ten years of his life; he brought her to a gala dinner hosted by the bank, they went to see a show and often spent much of their time walking around the city, hand in hand, basking in the closeness of the other. Every day, every spoken thought and conversation brought them closer, the connection between them, their relationship deepening in its intensity, and they both revelled in it. As they held each other tightly, in the quiet afterglow of their intimate nights together, with tears in their eyes at the thought of it, they discussed their upcoming parting.

"Charlie, when will I see you again?"

"Michael, my darling, yes, I want to see you again. Can I make that happen? The answer to that is also yes. Can presupposes want and both have to be in agreement. If we both want this, Michael, then we can both make it happen."

Michael, smiling in wondrous amazement at her ability to understand his underlying, unspoken thought, said, "Charlie, I want this, I want to see you again, and I, we, can make this happen."

Her only answer was to pull him closer to her, and then she kissed him slowly and tenderly, savouring the taste and sensation of him.

They talked about their future together, and of their own individual plans. Charlie talked about her plans to expand her business outside of London but that the when and where evaded her. Michael had already told her of his plan to leave the bank, and go back to painting full time but that the when also evaded him.

Both understood and acknowledged the importance of the other's individual plans and circumstances, and their mutual need for time. Michael needed time to adjust to life after his second divorce, and Charlie for her upcoming move to London and her growing business. However, they agreed that no matter what was happening in their lives, despite the distance they would make time for, support and above all celebrate each other.

A few days later, as they prepared to part at the airport, he wrapped her body close to his, kissed her lips and forehead.

"Charlie, I cannot wait to start painting you."

"And I cannot wait to meet her."

Before Charlie left his tight, warm embrace to get her flight to Dublin, she said, "Michael, my darling, we are both leaving London with something far more enjoyable, more pleasurable, and more valuable than anything we had before we arrived, and that is the knowledge of you, of I, of us."

As he was boarding his flight back to California, his phone pinged with a message from Charlie which said, 'By the way, my full name is Charlotte (smiley face) ... thought you might want to know that about me. Have a pleasant flight.'

In the months that followed their week together in London, Charlie had moved her business to London and had settled into her new home outside the city. Michael adjusted to his new life, and though still working for the bank, he spent more and more of his time painting, the subject for which he found was her, intricate details of her, his best friend and very beautiful muse.

Though they could not talk to each other every day, they communicated by all available means. They supposed that if military personnel, often thousands of miles away from their loved ones for months on end, or astronauts on the space station were able to nurture and maintain their relationships remotely, there was nothing to stop them from doing the same, and being creative in how they did so. It was an adventure for both of them, one which they welcomed and relished. By phone and video calls, email, and text messages, they laughed, joked and talked about everything, their work, the challenges they were facing, individually, professionally and as a couple.

Michael gave her a guided tour of his art studio, and she gave him a guided tour of her house and her neighbourhood outside London. Charlie would call him early in the morning London time and read to him bedtime story extracts from their favourite novels. He tried to teach her how to paint, which was far easier said than done, when neither could stop laughing or talking, long enough to concentrate. They celebrated Christmas and felt the pang of separation when it was time to open their gifts from each other. They celebrated a brand-New Year remotely, their wish, to and for each other, that it would be the only New Year which they would be apart for.

With a growing desire to be together, they both flew to New York to spend a week together. Touring the city, they picked up where they had left off in London, as if they had never been apart. Their love, for themselves and one another, grew and deepened with every step they took together, their parting in New York, much harder than it was the first time in London.

When Charlie had surprised him and told him that when she got back from New York, she had initiated the immigration process to the United States, Michael, to surprise her, had flown to London and stayed with her for a fortnight. The sheer pleasure which she derived from seeing him, making love to him, feeling the weight of him beside her, in her own bed, was blissful luxury to her. When she told him how she felt and why, Michael answered, "I love you too, Charlie."

Simple things like having breakfast, preparing and enjoying meals together, going places together, and sharing time and space was simply divine to them both.

In early summer, Charlie flew to him in Pasadena, California, to stay there for as long as travel rules would permit. As much as Charlie adored the vibrant and bustling nature of London, she fell in love with California. With an economy of its own larger than most countries, no matter where looked she saw growth, and opportunity, and that was before she had even landed.

Michael laughed as he picked her up from the airport, her piercing blue eyes radiant as she described all that she had seen and thought about from the air. As he drove to their home in Pasadena, Michael, joyous at the beautiful sight of her sitting beside him in the passenger seat of his car, absorbing everything that she saw around her, put his foot on the accelerator and picked up speed.

She noticed the roar of the turbo engine as he did so,

and said, "I cannot wait to get you home either." Home was a beautiful bungalow, with a lush green lawn, in a quiet picturesque neighbourhood of Pasadena. Michael parked, switched off the car, gently turned her face to him, and then kissed her deeply.

"This is, for us, for now, home, Charlie."

Charlie suddenly lost for words, felt a well of tears form in her eyes.

He tenderly kissed her forehead, wiped away the tear he saw falling down her cheek and almost in a whisper said, "That you are finally here Charlie, home, with me, is something I did not think possible or probable. I have spent much of my life forging my own path, and following my own direction, as you have yours but now, the only direction I want to go in is with you. We have come a long way, my darling, in our own way, for our own reasons, for our own benefit. We still have a long way to go, but if there is one thing I know without question, it is this: beyond my own life, my darling Charlie, you are the only way, the only reason, the only benefit that matters to me."

"I know, my love."

Her luggage in hand, Michael guided her to the door of their home and opened it. Entering, she saw the open plan living area, which led to a vast kitchen. At the back of the house was a beautiful expanse of garden, and then off in the distance, she saw the backdrop of canyons, mountains, and beautifully slanted terrain.

Michael, his eyes bright with joy to be with her, and have her here in his home, theirs now, followed and watched as she explored the house, her beautiful hands softly touching the various surfaces, fixtures, furniture, books, instruments, and ornaments that were positioned around the house.

She gazed with reverence at the artwork on the walls, noting the majority of it was his. Many times, previously, she had asked why he had not yet opened a gallery or started to sell his work. Seeing some of it now, up close and in person, she asked him again.

He said, "I have sold some pieces over the years, but I do not know if enough people would be interested in my artwork to buy it, and for me to make a living doing so."

Charlie, who was gazing at his exquisitely portrayed painting of a pair of eyes, hers, she surmised, turned to him and said, "Michael, my darling, if, by your statement, you have little experience of showing, or selling, you or your work to the public, then how do you know that they would not buy it, or what they would pay for it? Or are you expecting that people will automatically come to see you, without you, first, having to make yourself known to them? If so, that can only be achieved by you, even partially at least, going to them or finding a way of bringing them to you."

As she turned her gaze back around to the painting of the eyes, she continued, "You are not the first, my love, nor will you be the last person who has struggled to see and make that connection or to understand the cause of it. Your love of, and passion for, your work, your art, has been your primary motivation. In your own words, you have forged the path that you have, following your own direction, for your own reasons, for your own benefit. It is that same motivation that will continue to power you forward for the rest of your life.

"You have not allowed doubt to forge your path for you, or to get in the way up to now. My love, I urge you not to use unknowns as both the measure and the tool of measurement. Do not choose to trust or believe any doubts you may have about your work now, without examining the root, the knowledge of that which underpins them; do not judge yourself or your work, until or unless you have evidence, tangible criteria of what it is you are judging yourself by, or for.

"I have done it myself, Michael, often being my own worst critic, seeing and accepting as a given my own criticism, my own doubts about myself, as a reason not to try, or not to do something, mistaking excuses for reasons, placing them in front of myself as hurdles, and then using those same hurdles as definitive measures. It took a long time to see that what I was really doing was measuring myself, my own worth, doing precisely as I just said, using doubt, uncertainty about myself as the measure, and the tool of measurement. I cannot wave or wipe away all of your doubts, nor you mine, but where I can help you to do so, my love, I will."

Michael, unable to take his eyes off of her, her brilliance and wisdom ringing in his ears, went to her as she stood facing him by the wall between the living room and the kitchen. His desire for her mounting, he knew he had to have her. She saw the fire in his eyes as he approached, the proof of it swelling as he pulled her body tight to his, his hands cupping her breasts, kissing her face, her neck, her lips, her body reacting to her own need and responding to his. When bare skin met bare skin, her back to the wall, he lifted her. There was no time to wait nor any need to. He moaned when he felt her tightness, the sound and movement of her urging him on until neither could take any more, her trembling, shuddering, powerful body answering his. Both exhilarated, yet spent and exhausted, he led her to bed, where they lay, in a close, tight, lovers' embrace, delighting in the feel, the touch, the real, the home of the other.

In the midst of the carefree, idle talk they were enjoying, Michael suddenly stopped and exclaimed, "Charlie, I have just thought of a name for your expanded business. Knowing the very brilliant woman who will be taking what she has already achieved, rebuilding and powering it as I do, I think the name is most fitting. Drumroll, please!"

Laughing, Charlie, on the wooden head of the bed, did a drumroll, and waited with bated breath until he said, "Endeavour."

Repeating the word out loud as she thought about it, leaning in to kiss him, she said, "Michael, we have work to do, we have both spent long enough designing the blueprint, and gathering what we need for the foundations and building cornerstones. It is time to start building. Us, your art, your art gallery and Endeavour it is."

Later that evening, Michael had shown her his entire collection of paintings which he had created over the years. Charlie did not know what the criteria for being an art expert was, or if she was one, but she thought that each piece was extraordinary, the collection of them magnificent, the most beautiful expressions of a beautiful world put on canvas that she had ever seen.

When he had admitted that he felt exposed by her seeing them, she went to him, pulled him close to her, kissed him deeply, then she removed all her clothes, followed by his and they made slow, tender love on the floor of his studio surrounded by and basking in all that he held precious in his life.

In the weeks following her arrival, Charlie and Michael settled into life together. In the hours he went to work at the bank, she caught up with her work, and her clients back in Europe. The difference in time zone suited her; she managed her workload, her team, and her clients efficiently, keeping herself and her consulting customers happy in the process.

Every chance she had, she set her focus on expanding Endeavour, and on Michael's gallery.

When she had told him that she would come up with a plan for how to bring his art to the public, he had asked her why she wanted to do that and at the same time as Endeavour. Her answer was though the situation may seem on the surface to be very different, the solution to it was not. The discovery, learning, lessons, knowledge gathered from one, would help with the other. In reverent love and admiration for her, her mind, and her way of working, he kissed her eyelids, her forehead, her head, her hands, ears, nose, and lips,

"Charlie, for years, I have used brushes and paint on canvas to express how I perceive the detail, the precise reality that is this world, the people, and objects in it. You, however, are not a work of art, Charlie.

"You, your body and mind, the entirety of you is living, thinking, breathing art and artist. Where I put paint and materials to use in my work, you put knowledge to use in yours. We both use our minds, our knowledge; the application and expression of it is different. By that I mean not only do you perceive detail much as I do, but you also take the components, the details of that detail apart, and you name them precisely, you see how to use them, and where. The beautiful simplicity of it, benevolent and good.

"I am not afraid for you, Charlie, but there are people in this world who will wonder about and question your success. They will ask you to tell them how you have done it, and why you are a success. You will tell them, but they will feel threatened by your answer, and they will either refuse to understand, or refuse to think about what it is they feel threatened by or why it is that you are right, and they are wrong. They will hate you and try to punish you when they see your indifference to what they claim to be right and wrong, for your refusal to care about or accept their lack of understanding, as your problem to solve. You and I will laugh on the day that happens, firstly because we both already know it will happen, and secondly, in the time it will take for them to realise that you are a threat to them, you and Endeavour will already have succeeded."

"I am not afraid either, Michael. I have faced that same situation many times. I am not immune to it, nor have I developed immunity for it, but I have better things to do with my time."

CHAPTER SIX - NEAR SIGHT

Michael had read thousands of business plans and credit applications over the many years of his career at the Pasadena headquarters of Capital Enterprise Bank which he was now president of. He had met with thousands of the applicants and had approved millions of dollars' worth of credit to many of them. He had come across many ideas, for new inventions, devices, and innovations in every field from computing, technology, science, medicine, fashion, and entertainment to engineering.

He had met women and men, from all walks of life, ages, and backgrounds, who had started and nurtured their business from their student dorms, their basements, attics, or garages, had given and risked everything they had in order to bring their idea to life.

He had met those who had demanded that the bank support their idea, even though they had no information to describe the idea, nor a plan for how the business could or would work, nor any evidence that might reasonably demonstrate an ability to repay the loan.

It was a very rare occasion that the business plan he was reading, and the idea contained in it, would stop him in his tracks because of its sheer brilliance. So rare an occurrence that he could still count the occasions on his two hands.

Sipping the delicious coffee that Charlie had made and put in a flask for him as was her custom in the time since she had arrived, Michael was sitting at the desk in his office, carefully reading through a business plan for a large credit application from a new technology company, which had been submitted by post to the bank. Due to the sum involved, and according to processes in place at the bank, the application had been sent directly to him for his review and approval. As he read it, he could see that it needed work, but that the underlying idea for the business was one of those truly rare occasions. He read the details provided about the applicant and followed up by methodically doing his own research online.

As the beginning of an idea formed in his mind, Michael read the plan again, made notes and by the time he had finished, the idea was clear. He picked up the phone, called his executive assistant and asked her to clear his schedule for the rest of the week. Then he called the number on the application and waited for it to be answered. As soon as it was, he said, "Good morning, I am Michael Weston, calling from Capital Enterprise Bank. I would like to speak to Jane Adams please."

"This is Jane speaking."

"Jane, I have just read your credit application, and your business plan. The idea is brilliant; however, the plan needs work. I am calling you directly because I have an idea, a proposal for you, which may seem unorthodox but will save you time and a whole lot of money and if it doesn't, it will make for one very unusual experience."

"Right, that is indeed very unusual, Michael, but please go on, I am listening."

He walked Jane through his proposal in meticulous detail.

By the end of the call an hour later, they were chatting like old friends. Before hanging up the call, she said, "Thank you, Michael. I have not enjoyed a phone call this much in a long time, and even more so, when the caller is from a bank."

Laughing back at her, he said, "I have messaged you with details for my address, and I will see you both soon."

Michael picked up his phone again and dialled another number. When he heard the voice answer, he said, "Hi, Sam, it's Michael Weston. I have a venture which I think you might be interested in, and a group of people I would like you to meet, one of whom is my girlfriend Charlie. If you are available, could you come over please?"

"Why yes, you caught me at a good time, I am at the tail end of a round of golf at the club, and you know I am not someone to pass on a venture without exploring it first," Sam replied.

"Splendid, Sam. I am confident you will find it to be worth your while."

"I will finish my game, and I should be there in twenty minutes."

"Wonderful, in which case, I will see you soon," Michael said, and went to the copier outside his office to make a second copy of the plan.

Michael hung up the phone with Sam and called Charlie. When she answered, concerned, and confused as to why he was calling her, and why he was doing so mid-morning, he said excitedly, "Charlie, my darling, all will be explained later. For now, however, there is something which you need to see, and then two people, actually three people, I would like you to meet. I will be home in fifteen minutes. We will have guests arriving. I will see you soon, my love."

As soon as Jane had finished the call with Michael, she raced to find her husband, and very excitedly she said, "David, you and I are going to Pasadena. Pack an overnight bag, we will be needing it."

David Banner watched his beautiful, brilliant wife, usually so composed, now so excited and so animated. He listened and went to pack a bag. In less than fifteen minutes, with bags packed, Jane and David were in the car and had started the drive from Escondido to Michael's address in Pasadena. Jane composed herself as she drove and explained to David what she and Michael had discussed. As they navigated traffic and got closer to Pasadena, they both felt the thrill of excitement and anticipation.

Charlie was still pondering why Michael had sounded so excited, and who he had invited to their home, when she heard his car pull up. Opening the front door of their home, she watched him get out of the car, paper files in his hand, and one of the widest grins she had ever seen on his face.

"Since when does that car fly?" she asked.

"I found a button, not sure what it was for, I pressed it, to my surprise the car took off."

He kissed her quickly, as he did so he heard, then saw a car driven by Samuel Walker pull up.

Michael went to meet him, shook his hand, and embraced Sam in welcome. In quick succession, Michael and Sam were standing at the front door of the house. Before Michael even had the chance to open his mouth to start introductions, Sam said, "As I live and breathe, you are Charlotte Rochford, owner of Value Signals

Consulting, right?"

"What? Why yes, indeed I am. Though I answer to Charlie, rather than Charlotte. Have we met before, do I know you?" she said, puzzled.

Her confusion was mirrored by Michael who said, "How on Earth, Sam?"

"No, you and I have not met before, you do not know me, but your reputation precedes you, Charlie. I have known that Michael has been in a relationship with a woman named Charlie, but I had no idea that woman is actually you, or that you have been here in California living with Michael, right on my doorstep.

"You see, I am a private investor with my own investment firm. By private investment I mean that I do not follow or trade the stock market. If, or when, I invest in a business or company, I do so on the basis of research and analysis of the business from its inception, achieved by evaluating financial records, reports and statements, meeting the owners, the people who work in the business, and seeing the business for myself.

"In the course of my work, both you, and your consulting firm have come up many times in reports and in meetings with the businesses in Europe and the United Kingdom that I invest in. With help from Peggy, my wife, we researched you and kept going until we found your picture in a newspaper article. I have not forgotten your face, as I was hoping that someday I would finally meet you.

"Charlie, your business has been of significant importance to mine, because though I could see the multiple layers of value in the businesses I was interested in, the owners could not or, in many cases, had lost sight of it. The work you did with those clients benefited their business, yours and mine. Your track record is quite a phenomenon, and I am more than happy to admit that you are a heroine of mine and of my wife, we are both long time admirers of your work. Now consider this bold if you wish, and of course I have questions, but whatever this venture is, which Michael predicted I would be interested in, I can say that as you are at the helm, I am in, but for now, what do we call it?"

Charlie said, "Well, Sam. It is a real pleasure to meet you and thank you on many counts. It seems that we have much to talk about. As for the name of the venture, it is called Endeavour."

Both laughed when Michael grinned and said, "Sam, I would like to introduce you to Charlie Rochford, and Charlie, this is Samuel Walker. I am a smart money man, Sam is even smarter, and all the more so, now that I know he was already aware of you. Seeing as my job here is done, and Sam, I have helped you realise a dream, let us get you some coffee and get you two caught up."

Over coffee, Charlie and Sam got to know each other, Charlie talked about her business, her vision for expansion of it, and Sam filled her in on his. He told her about his beautiful wife Peggy, a brilliant mind too, he said, when it came to understanding the nuts and bolts of a business.

As he showed Charlie pictures of Peggy, Charlie exclaimed, "Your wife is Margaret Sanders? The author?"

"Why, yes! The one and only Margaret Sanders. Do you know her?" Sam asked.

"I have read all of her brilliant books, cover to cover several times, and as much as you have always wanted to meet me, I have always wanted to meet Margaret, or should I say Peggy."

"Well, I can assure you, Charlie, Peggy has always wanted to meet you too! Wow, what a stupendous day today has already been and it is still only barely afternoon. Let me call Peggy and see if she is free to come down here too, and if possible, turn this incredible day into a truly extraordinary one."

Sam picked up his phone and called Peggy. Though she was busy writing when she answered his call, when he explained where he was, and with whom, without hesitation she said she would be at Michael's address in fifteen minutes.

While they waited for Peggy to arrive, Charlie learned that Sam and Michael knew each other from when they had both worked for the bank and had remained friends ever since. To her delight, she discovered that Sam had been encouraging Michael to open his art gallery, in fact Sam had been one of Michael's artwork customers. She made a note when Sam suggested looking at La Jolla as a place to set up a gallery and invited them both to use his beach house there as a means of checking out the area.

When Michael had a message from Jane to say that they were about forty minutes away, he interrupted Sam and Charlie who were deep in conversation about their mutual clients, and how it was they had not met before. He handed them a paper file each and said, "You both need to read this."

Curiosity piqued, they each opened what Michael had given them and began to read.

It was a business plan for a technology company, co-founders Jane Adams, the technologist, and her husband David Banner, a recruitment consultant with his own firm. The business specialised in quantum computing, cyber technology, blockchain, data engineering, artificial intelligence, process automation and analytics, the core of which was SAI, an exascale supercomputer, the limbs of SAI, a blockchain and artificial intelligence system.

The plan laid out how each of the services would be provisioned in order to generate revenue. They noted upfront costs were high, the largest of which came from recruitment, and resourcing. Charlie and Sam evaluated the financial projections, from infrastructure build and run, to ongoing operations costs which considered everything from energy usage to postage stamps. They examined the sales and marketing strategy, target markets, clients and revenue streams.

Charlie made no sound whatsoever as she assembled thoughts in her mind. She read it a second time, thinking, shaping, imagining, visualising, and all the while updating her mental notes. Exhilarated by what she had read, a plan was formed in her head.

"This woman, Jane Adams, is a genius. I really want to meet her."

"So do I," Sam said, and added, "The core idea is the product of a genius, and though that plan is detailed, aggressive and ambitious, it will not work on its own".

Charlie, thrilled to have Sam articulate precisely what she had also concluded, said, "It will not work, but I know how to make it work."

Michael, with a wide grin said, "I am very glad that you both want to meet her because she and David are on their way here right now."

"What? How? Why?" they chorused.

"Well, as you both know, I have worked at the bank for well over twenty-five years. In that time, I have seen thousands of business ideas, many of them good, and just as many bad ones. I can count on my own two hands the number of them which were truly exceptional, and were as you describe, 'the product of genius'.

"I read through Jane's plan this morning. I also identified the concept as brilliant but as you have both concluded, the plan needs work, a lot of it. So I called Jane, and explained to her what it was that needed work, and that though the idea was sound, the bank could not approve the finance based upon the plan.

"I then told her about you, Charlie, the very beautiful architect of Endeavour, who I knew, would see the idea for what it is, and then create a plan which will in fact, and for good reason, work. I then called Sam who I rightly predicted would be interested too. Long story short, in about forty minutes or so Jane and David will be here to meet us."

Charlie, unusually speechless, collected her thoughts and composed herself. She pulled Michael to her, affectionately hugged and kissed him and said, "Thank you, Michael."

Then the doorbell rang and at the same time, Sam's phone pinged with a message from Peggy to say that she had arrived, so Sam, with a nod from Michael and Charlie went to open the door. Sam, returning to the kitchen with Peggy, said, "Charlie, this is my beautiful wife Peggy, and Peggy, this is the one and only Charlie Rochford."

Charlie and Peggy shook hands, and hugged each other, revelling in the delight of finally meeting each other.

While Peggy briefed herself with the business plan, Charlie, Michael and Sam kept chatting, until they heard the ping of Michael's phone signalling that a message had landed, which he read and then said, "They are here."

****

Jane Adams, and her husband David Banner, had pulled up outside the home of two strangers. Several times on the drive, they had both discussed if they and the people they were about to meet were crazy.

When they had submitted the credit application and business plan to the bank, neither could have predicted, in a thousand years, that they would now be parked outside the house of the president of that bank, with little information about what they were doing there, except that which she had learned from the telephone conversation she had with Michael, only a few hours earlier.

David laughed when she compared the peculiar event unfolding to what happens when one is writing code for a computer program and an incorrect placement of a bracket or semicolon could cause any number of unexpected issues in the application.

Jane laughed and agreed when he compared the event to his work in his recruitment firm, where he could see the potential of the candidate, but they had not communicated it very well. They also agreed that over the course of their work, they were no strangers to taking risks in the pursuit of new opportunities that would enhance and improve their lives.

Jane, before they got out of the car, turned to David, and kissed him.

"Here is to the next one."

Michael was excited as he opened the front door. With Charlie, Sam, and Peggy behind him they walked down the front steps and went to meet Jane and David. With a broad welcoming smile, he extended his hand toward the tall, slender, blonde-haired woman, and they shook hands, and he said, "Welcome, Jane. It is truly a pleasure to meet you, to put a face to the name, and particularly so soon after speaking with you."

He turned his attention to David, they shook hands and Michael said, "Hi, David, I am Michael. It is a pleasure to meet you, and I thank you, very much, for coming with Jane.

"I would first like to introduce you to Charlie Rochford. Charlie is many wonderful, beautiful things to me, but for now, for both of you, for you, Jane, she is the reason that I asked you here today. I would also like to introduce you to Samuel Walker, an investor, and his wife Peggy, both good friends of mine, and two long time admirers of Charlie's work. I called Sam, right after I hung up the phone from you, and asked if he would like to come over to find out more. Peggy is here because Charlie has been a long time fan of Peggy's books on business and business operations.

"So this opportunity here seemed like a perfect occasion for everyone to meet and be part of the same conversation with you and David. In any case, here we all are, and Sam, Charlie and Peggy have all read your plan."

Peggy extended her hand in turn to Jane and David, who both introduced themselves, and then Sam followed by shaking hands and greeting them both too.

Charlie smiled, shook hands with both of them and offered them a warm welcome.

"Jane, David, thank you very much for coming, even though I imagine you must both have wondered and discussed at length if you were crazy for doing so."

David, with a grin, said, "You got that right, Charlie! I am quite used to crazy ideas from my wife, but the idea of driving to meet two strangers sounded bonkers to me too. It is wonderful to meet you, Sam, Peggy and of course, Michael."

Jane laughed, and said, "David is right on all counts, Charlie. It is a pleasure to meet you, and all of you."

Michael, with an easy smile back to Jane, said, "Charlie, Peggy and Sam have all read your plan, so let's get you settled after your drive up here and bring this plan to life. I hope you brought your overnight bags, Jane?"

"We did."

David chatted with Peggy and Michael, and Jane with Charlie and Sam as they walked up the front steps and into the house. As they each took a seat on the tall stools around the island in the kitchen, and enjoyed coffee together, the six of them learned more about each other.

Charlie told them about herself, her business, and her work. Michael described how Charlie and he had met in London, his work at the bank and that his true passion in life was painting as he gestured to the walls around them.

Jane described how she and David had met not long after they had graduated university. She talked passionately about her love of mathematics, physics, engineering and technology, her career in technology and that it was the only work she ever wanted to do and that it led her to Sai, the supercomputer artificial intelligence and blockchain system which she had architected and designed, a working prototype of. David talked about his career in human resources and recruitment, then about his own business as a recruitment agent, his love of playing drums, guitar and composing songs.

Sam told Jane and David about himself and replayed why he had wanted to meet Charlie for a long time, and he thanked them both for being the reason why Michael had called him. Peggy echoed Sam in her wish to meet Charlie and then she told them about her career in operations spanning many decades, where she had also fostered a love of innovation and progress through automation, robotic processes and the future of artificial intelligence and blockchain in business operations, which was how she had come to discover her love of, and passion for, writing books on the subject.

Jane, eager anticipation in her voice, said, "Peggy, Charlie, I very much look forward to hearing both of your thoughts on improving operations with technology, and specifically with Sai, and I cannot wait to discover even more business use case opportunities with it. David and I have already identified many, though admittedly we have been looking at operations and applications from the outside in, rather than from the inside out. Michael told me you have all read the business plan, what did you all think of it?"

Charlie replied, "Jane, I think the idea is brilliant, even more so having learned more about Sai from you just now. However, unless you can treble your sales forecasts or you have vast sums of money at your disposal for the next five years, the plan will not work. It will not work because the plan is undervaluing the two very things which underpin your whole idea, the technology itself and knowledge. It has highlighted the usual high costs and expenses around recruiting and retaining the highly skilled and experienced talent you need for building the systems, applications and other technology you want around Sai, without considering who that technology is going to be used by, for what purpose, if it could be repurposed, and in how many ways, or that the people to be recruited actually have the right knowledge they will need to understand, not just how to technically build or run something but understand precisely what it will be doing, processing, or outputting, as and when it runs. You, yourself just alluded to the gap in your plan when you said you have been looking at use cases from the outside in."

Sam added, "Charlie is right, and there are ways, Jane, to put the correct value against the most valuable parts of the idea, the technology and the knowledge. Doing so will be more efficient, less expensive, more productive, and above all, more profitable. The only way of achieving it, however, does not fit under a common practice way of running a business."

Peggy added, "Sam and Charlie are both right, Jane. Your idea is brilliant, the product of a brilliant mind. Do not limit yourself to common, or what might be called normal practices. If you do, you are limiting yourself. If both you and David will permit us, Charlie, Sam and I can prove it."

Jane, as her logical mind processed every thought and word, glanced briefly at her husband. She saw the look of deep respect and admiration on his face toward Charlie, Sam and Peggy, as he was staring at them, his attention alternating between them, listening intently, digesting every gesture, facial expression, each word spoken by both of them. Jane, rarely overcome by emotion in front of anyone who was not her husband, found that she was now.

She examined what she was feeling and identified a very deep sense of relief, of freedom, and then joy. It was, she thought, as if Charlie by her words, Sam and Peggy with theirs, had wrapped her up in a warm, comforting hug in which all one can do is exhale deeply.

"David, may I hug your wife please? I think she is in need of it."

"She does, you may, but only if I get one after, Charlie."

Charlie stood, went to Jane and opened her arms wide, and the women embraced.

Jane said, "Michael, lest I should forget to thank you later, I would very much like to thank you now.

"Charlie, Sam, and Peggy, I know that we have much to learn about each other, but I can tell you now that I have always enjoyed working with technology, often more than I have with people. I enjoy technology because it requires deep logic, reason, knowledge, understanding, facts, and evidence in order to work. There is little place for emotions or feelings of any kind, unless that is, I have spent weeks or months writing code for a programme which had worked yesterday but then inexplicably does not.

"What struck me most about the call I had with Michael earlier today was that he presented his reasons for the bank not approving the credit application, in a clear, logical and reason-oriented way. He went a step further, of course, than I imagine most banks or certainly bank presidents would in that he had an alternative solution ready. That Michael did the first part was a pleasant shock; then that he did the last part struck me, like a pleasant bolt of lightning, so rare an occasion it truly is to find someone, apart from my husband, who does either."

Jane paused for a moment, and said, "Charlie, Sam and Peggy, when you each spoke just now, I was more overwhelmed by how you said what you said, by which I mean the open, clear and logical way in which you said it. Charlie, that you understood the effect on me was just as rare a treasure to find. I cannot speak for David, but I know that though we have barely scratched the surface, we will be friends for a very long time. A gift like that is, on its own, something I never thought I would find. I am deeply grateful to you Michael, for bringing us here, to you Charlie and both of you, Peggy and Sam."

David, with a look of pure tenderness towards his wife, turned his attention back to Charlie, Michael, Sam and Peggy, and said, "It is indeed a rare occurrence for me as much as it is for Jane. I am grateful to you all. Now, Charlie, where is my hug? And then, we would love to hear your plan."

Charlie laughed, then reached out to David, and gave him as open and large a hug, as she had to Jane.

They all laughed, and more hugs were shared and exchanged when Sam said, "I would love a hug, and I give great hugs too."

Before they ventured into Charlie's plan, all agreed they were hungry so Charlie and Michael prepared lunch for the six of them. As they sat down to enjoy it together, they chatted as if they had known each other for years, delightfully comfortable in each other's presence.

Getting around to business, Charlie began to articulate a plan to bring Jane's idea and her own business together, and turn both into a set of viable, productive, and profitable businesses, of which David with his background and business in recruitment, Peggy with hers, and Sam with his, were all, pending their agreement, fundamental parts.

Jane looked at David, an unspoken question passing between them. She said, "Charlie, before you go on, what do we call it?"

"We call it Endeavour," Sam and Michael chorused.

Charlie explained that the first part of the business was a life skills and training academy, the purpose of which was twofold: to begin to solve longer term talent pursuit needs for the business; and to generate income for Endeavour in the short and medium terms but in a strategic and cost-effective way. She explained that they, or David, in particular, already had the resources available to begin to find the coaches and the students for the academy.

"What resources?" David asked.

"Well, David, for the people that you have dealt with over the years in your own recruitment firm, have you kept and stored their information?"

He answered, "Yes I have. All my records are stored in a secure blockchain distributed database, which Jane created and manages for me. It was one of her first use case tests for advanced blockchain technology, and of course for Sai. It has been fantastic for me and each of the individual clients who use my firm, for the purposes of storing and protecting their personal data in a transparent, auditable way, when it is shared with one, or more, potential or even previous employers, while also tracking the candidates progression through the recruitment, contracting, onboarding and probation processes in a tamper proof, immutable way, even more so for temporary, agency or short contract roles or for candidates who are working multiple jobs concurrently.

"When my clients sign up to use my firm, and periodically thereafter, we go through a lengthy data privacy, permissions and usage review process. Regular updates are shared with each client so they can see, have access and control over their own data, from what is shared, where, how and with whom and who it can then be used by."

"Excellent! That alone is a powerful proof of your plan, Jane! That is the resource we will start with, mindful of data protection and privacy guidelines. The database which enables your business, David, is a goldmine, as it is precisely where we will find the teachers and students we need for the academy."

"I do not understand," David said.

It was Michael who said, "David, as Charlie, and Sam, both said right at the beginning, a plan for a business that undervalues the very things that underpin and power it will not truly tap into its full potential.

"You have worked in recruitment, and I, with Sam in banking and investments, for years. We have between us, I am sure, seen perhaps thousands of businesspeople who think that to succeed in business means putting vast numbers of people on their payroll in order to achieve its goal and mission. They come to you to find the resources, then they come to the bank, or to an investor like Sam, looking for the capital to pay for them. When you ask them for a profile of the candidates they want, they give you a vague description, and an equally vague checklist of arbitrary qualities: someone who will fit into the culture, a team player, punctual, organised, experienced, and skilled at whatever function they think a person in that role should have. When you ask them why so many resources are needed, and if they have the budget to pay for them, they talk about not being able to keep people, their high staff turnover, and budget constraints.

"That is true, Michael, most of my business is a result of it," David affirmed.

Michael continued, "When I ask why so many resources are needed, and how the business plans to pay for them, I am often met with hostility, and told that bringing more people onto payroll will bring in more sales, or that a successful company these days is more about their reputation as an employer than the amount of profit generated. I am certain that you have seen as many as I have and have been a creditor of these businesses, which somehow manage to limp along, for a while surviving on taxpayer funded subsidies, their employees not only afraid for their jobs, but are paying in both their time and tax to support the very company they work for, or else the business fails.

"Indeed, that is so, Michael, and I have been burned many times."

"However, for all those failures, David, I am sure you have come across the truly successful entrepreneurs and businesspeople who succeed because they have identified through discovery, by doing that work, precisely what resources are needed and why. They understand how to use and innovate with as few resources as possible, in order to achieve their primary goal, which is to grow their business, to make a profit, by means of exchanging value for value.

"There are many reasons why these people succeed, but I have found the primary one is that when they started out, they performed, out of necessity, all of the work of every role and function which they then recruited for themselves. The consequence of which is they understand what each role or function is, its value and purpose in and to the overall business. Furthermore, by understanding the value of the work done in that job, they understand the price they are willing to pay for it, that price being what will be paid to the person who will be hired to do it, and not necessarily at the lowest price either."

Both Charlie and Peggy nodded in agreement with Michael, and then Peggy added, "To add to Michael's statement, you have, David, perhaps more than anyone else in this room, met as many good candidates and employees as you have bad ones. The good ones are often overlooked because they do not quite fit the prescribed checklist, or are not loud, bold, or confident enough to make themselves seen, yet these are the very people who are most often the hard workers, the fixers of problems in a business, the real experts on what the business is, does, and what does and does not work."

Charlie continued by saying, "Such individuals thrive in situations where they have to think for themselves, to do, for their own benefit and purpose, either profit or experience, the work in the role they are employed for, that they do it is the value they cherish and that is what they are trading in exchange for wages. The database is a goldmine, the data within it is the gold because it has stored information about the very people who would be needed to establish, build, and run a successful company, with the rule book of common practice thrown in the bin.

"There is no shortage of talented, skilled, self-motivated, productive, and passionate individuals out there in the world. That database will prove it, and the academy will be the way in which these individuals will surface themselves."

David said, "I like your way of thinking and I also really need to throw my own rule book in the bin. You are right Charlie."

Charlie nodded in agreement and proceeded to articulate how

the business starting with the academy would begin to generate income, achieved by providing chargeable day or evening courses, to the public. The courses would, initially, be aimed at life skills, the types often not taught in the traditional education system. She gave some examples: tax returns, cooking on a budget, nutrition, basic computer skills, managing home budgets. The range of courses would, over time, expand into other areas like technology, data science, business administration, or setting up a business.

She explained that people paying for courses at the academy would be doing far more for themselves than just furthering their education; they would be investing in themselves by demonstrating an interest in themselves, by doing something for themselves. "It is those people who want to do more with their lives to find a purpose or new direction, but through whatever circumstances – redundancy, age, inexperience, being overlooked in their current job, or for reasons of their self-confidence – have not been able to redirect their purpose, but when they see an opportunity to do so, they take it. That is true for both the coaches and the students.

"Ultimately, the academy will bring people to Endeavour, in doing so, that will provide us with an income stream, and our business with the means of identifying the talent we will need to operate all parts of Endeavour, but also coaches and students alike will have the opportunity to use their reshaped or enhanced skills, talents and value to supply and provide services to the enterprise and trade centre where small or medium business owners and traders can run their businesses from, as a means of keeping overheads down but have direct access to a large pool of consumers, each other of course and we have a potential pool of our target customers under our roof.

"The traders will be charged, but not as much as they will have to pay if they go elsewhere or try to keep their business running and growing from their basements or own premises. The students from the academy may even want to become a trader or small business owner in their own right. We will provide the conditions that could make that opportunity possible to them if they want to take it.

"Once established," Charlie explained, "there would be a suite of other business services, run as the Endeavour Operations arm, which will provide services inwards to our business, and outwards to those businesses in the enterprise centre, and to other companies. For example, the finance department will manage payroll, procurement, capital finance, file tax returns, procure insurance, manage accounts, and set investment strategies for Endeavour; those same services will be provided by Endeavour to businesses in the enterprise and trade centre and externally to my existing clients for instance and others. Endeavour will have a customer service function for itself, which can also be provided as a service to businesses in the enterprise centre. The technology arm will be extended for use as a paid service to our customers in the enterprise centre and beyond in varying capacities, application development, integrations, migrations, business processing and more. Sai will largely be used to perform routine Endeavour operational tasks, while we are working in the business, guiding, building, and shaping the business and our training, testing and governance of Sai and the truly invaluable blockchain component."

Charlie and Peggy discussed the merits of various operating models and agreed that they were not going to run Endeavour as a lean operation by spending months of time or resources understanding and mapping the company's value. "We know what our value is, where it comes from and how to optimise it. Do we need a clear visual understanding, a test plan if you will, of how Endeavour will operate? Yes. Do we want to document in granular detail, all the steps in all the processes that might go with that? Perhaps, but only where it is done on an end-to-end basis, and is used to serve as a baseline guide, for the individuals, namely us, and our people and Sai, to learn about, to know and understand the entire business, both our own and that of our customers inside and out."

Charlie explained how otherwise, as she had observed many times with her clients, Endeavour would run a risk of tying the business to fixed ways of working, which might be helpful for the purposes of ticking a box to say the company had processes in place for individuals to follow but in using fixed, rigid processes, this would limit innovation, growth, change and only serve to mask the key components of Endeavours value, and limit the individuals in the business and limit Sai in being able to understand and map how a process change in one area will affect others, in terms of both time and cost..

Sam, Peggy, Jane, David all asked questions as did Michael who was just as rigorous in his examination of the idea and Charlie's thought process. As Charlie answered each one, they understood the extent of her genius, the brilliance of her mind, of her way of working, and the full chain of ideas, which she had so expertly and efficiently overlaid on top of Jane's to articulate the full scope and scale of the business. They grasped how and why the merged idea would work, and they all agreed that it was a novel way of running a business.

Sam, in particular, fully comprehended why Charlie's existing business was so successful and why her reputation had followed her around the world and he, in particular, could not wait to work with her. He told her so. Peggy was vocally excited by the possibility, given the opportunity and agreement to write a new book about Charlie, Endeavour and the large-scale operation which they would be running.

Jane, who for her own comprehension needed to play back what she had heard so far from Charlie to herself and in her own way, asked, "Are you saying that we would be building, and running the entire company as if it were a network on an integrated software application but with a twist?

"By that I mean, understand the business areas, and the users in that area that will be using it and why. Before putting any data or information into it, consider how to enable each business area, to be aware of what the other is doing, and why because if they are not aware, that will affect the data, the information which will be stored in and processed through it. Once we have done all that, we then automate it, enabling us to sell the application inwards and outwards and at scale?"

Charlie, with profound admiration for how Jane had posed the question, thought about it for a moment, then she smiled and said, "Yes, and the key to it is Sai. We know that supercomputer technology, blockchain and advances in artificial intelligence have played, and will continue to play, a significant role in changing what and how companies operate, particularly in respect to their people, through automating more and more tasks. There is an assumption that artificial intelligence will replace people but, Jane, correct me if I am wrong, that assumption is a very large error in understanding how artificial intelligence is developed, how it is trained, tested, and how the output from it is validated and used correctly.

"This might also seem like a far-fetched statement, Jane, but have you explored the possibility of how to make artificial intelligence sentient? I imagine the thought has crossed your mind as much as it has crossed mine, though it's a conversation for another time perhaps."

Jane, with deep admiration for the astute observation made by Charlie, said, "You are correct, Charlie. Artificial Intelligence is a buzzword and like many such words, there is little understanding of what is actually required to make artificial intelligence, including generative language models, work, and do so more effectively than it can today. Sai is proof of it.

"The reason that I required so many resources in my business plan was because Sai will require very specific types of skills, and therefore people to not only enhance what I have already built but to continue training, testing, validating and retraining it and tuning Sai's output, going from supervised, to unsupervised to deep learning mode over time.

"Your statement on sentient artificial intelligence is not outlandish, I have explored the concept of sentience, and I have a theory on how to progress it in respect to Sai, so yes I very much look forward to that conversation with you."

Peggy was amazed by the potential scale and ease of operations she saw in Endeavour; she had written books along the lines of what Charlie's new model was, but her books had not explored the depth of possibility which Charlie and Jane had just articulated.

David, as he listened to every word, and thought about every detail, could already visualise the academy, the enterprise centre and resourcing for both. Though there would be a huge amount of work to do, he found that the simplicity of the overall business and the potential he saw in it amazed him, and in itself, powered him. He said, "Charlie, you are an incredible woman, and I hope you, or Michael don't mind me saying so, but I think I have fallen in love with you a little."

Jane smiled toward her husband, then toward Charlie and said, "He actually has, Charlie, I can see it on his face. I know why though, and I feel it too."

Charlie answered, "I know and it is mutual, I can assure you both."

Sam echoed David and Jane and said, "Charlie, I have admired, respected and loved you, from afar for a long time, but it is only now that I know why that is."

"David, Jane, and Sam, I fell in love with Charlie, mere seconds after she made me jump out of my skin, by the elevator in London. I cannot say I blame you now. I am surprised it took you this long to admit it."

Charlie laughed, thanked them all for the expressions of love, admiration and respect and then continued on to explain how she would move her existing business under Endeavour. They discussed how the business would be structured and financed, by way of a private wholly owned holding company, to form a private corporate group where Jane, David, Sam and Peggy, and the other Endeavour partners they would soon find, could transfer and run their own businesses within Endeavour.

Jane picked up the mantle from Charlie by saying that Endeavour Technology would build, run and supply the infrastructure and technology services for all parts of the business. She added that she would make a small fortune, both in time and money, because for the first time in her life, she could do it properly, her own way, using the exascale supercomputer, blockchain and artificial intelligence system, named Sai, which she had designed, engineered, built, developed, tested and named, as if it were a child, and which in many ways it was to her.

The first task for Sai would be to work on that database and begin mining for the gold contained within it. The second task would be, they agreed, to find temporary premises for Endeavour, and of course for Charlie to complete her relocation from the United Kingdom to the United States.

Charlie, to articulate the extent of her ambition for Endeavour, said, "Jane, Sam, David, Peggy, when we have established a permanent home for Endeavour, it will become the headquarters. The headquarters of what, you may ask. The answer is, we will replicate Endeavour in other parts of this country and eventually abroad."

With a loving, knowing smile toward Michael, she said,

"Michael, I am not excluding you from this part but I hope that you by then, my love, will have opened your gallery and the only thoughts of endeavour in your mind will be your next painting."

"Hear, hear!" said Sam, who was busy thinking about who he knew to bring in as Endeavour partners. He and Peggy made some suggestions, and with agreement from Charlie, Michael, Jane and David, suggested that he and Peggy would leave them for the evening, to make some calls to those very people. Before leaving, Peggy and Sam invited everyone to their house for brunch in the morning, for what they hoped might be the very first Endeavour board meeting. As Peggy and Sam moved to leave them, hugging each of them before they left, Sam admitted that he had not felt so excited by a venture in a long time, his admission acknowledged and shared by all of them.

When Jane and David confirmed they would indeed stay the night, Charlie and Jane prepared the guest room, and left Michael and David to make a delicious dinner, which they enjoyed around the beautiful antique wooden dining table. As they dined, they talked about Michael's artwork and his plans for his gallery.

David said, "Michael, you talked about the goldmine of value I have been storing up. You have been storing up your own. So, I say, it is high time you put yours to work for you. We will back you, as you have backed us here today."

Jane added, "David is right, Michael. Endeavour will work without you; you have worked too long and hard over the years towards your own objective to say otherwise. You have brought us here together which has enabled us to realise our goal for which we will be forever grateful. Now it is time to realise your own."

Charlie, with gratitude toward David and Jane, and pride and love to Michael, said, "Thank you, David, and Jane, from the bottom of my heart.

When they retired to the comfortable, relaxed living room after dinner, the conversation turned to what Charlie had seen and thought of California so far, and how it compared to London. There was no comparison, she said, and the weather was decidedly better. She and Michael had toured up the coast of northern California to visit Michael's parents and family but had not yet ventured further south. Charlie, thinking back to the mental note she had made when Sam had recommended La Jolla as a place to set up an art gallery, said that she and Michael were overdue a trip further south, to the delight of Jane and David who lived just south of Escondido.

Many conversations covering many topics later, the four of them, exhausted by excitement and anticipation for all that lay ahead for them, said goodnight to each other and retired to their rooms. Once strangers at the start of the day, they were close friends and business partners by the end of it.

As Charlie and Michael lay together in a warm, tight embrace in their bed, they laughed, celebrated, and talked about the day just gone, the love, happiness and pride they felt for both themselves and each other in their individual and mutual accomplishments. She kissed him delicately on his soft lips and said, "I know without question too, my darling Michael, that beyond my own life, you are the only way, the only reason, the only benefit that matters to me."

To hear his own words played back to him, and her beautiful lilting voice saying them were, to his ears, even sweeter than usual. He kissed her and said, "I love you, Charlie. Goodnight, my darling."

Jane and David, curled up close together in their bed in the guest room, were also digesting the events of the day, from the phone call she had received from Michael to the overwhelming recognition that their way of looking at the world, their love of it, was not isolated to them. They had met four other brilliant minds, truly magnificent individuals who not only shared a different way of thinking, of seeing the possible in the impossible, but embraced it as much as they did.

When Sam and Peggy had both arrived at their home, he gently pulled her close to him, kissed her, and though there was no music playing, proceeded to dance with her around their living room. As they danced, they talked about Charlie, Jane, David and the prospect of Endeavour. They considered both their professional experiences and all the adventures they had been on together, and then Peggy said, "Sam, Endeavour is the ultimate venture, the sum of all that we have both been working towards, in our own way. You and your investment company and I, over the course of my career, in pursuit of my own passion in life, material for the books which I have lovingly written and published on the very subject, which we can now actually put a name to: "Endeavour."

"You wise and beautiful woman, Peggy. I did not think it was possible to love and adore you even more than I already do, and yet here I am finding that I do," said Sam, kissing her forehead, the face and moving to her lips.

She smiled at him, kissed him back and said, "Before we get distracted and carried away with each other, Sam, we need to call Devon and Amy and then call Louisa and Andrea. They are the perfect fit with Endeavour. Charlie, Michael, Jane and David will, I am certain, see and love their value as much as we do. Endeavour will most definitely be needing Amy Forsyth; she is the best organisational, occupational psychologist out there and one of the smartest minds I have ever come across. Devon, Andrea and Louisa are exceptional at what they do, and will be in excellent company with Charlie, Jane and David and make up a company of minds that will truly be a force to be reckoned with."

And so, Peggy and Sam, powered by the prospect of the venture that lay ahead, at the helm of which would be Charlie Rochford, the most brilliant mind that either of them had ever encountered, contacted the two couples. By the end of the conversations with Devon, Amy, Louisa and Andrea, with realised excitement, ten people went to sleep that night, in eager anticipation of a bold and bright new venture in their near sight.

CHAPTER SEVEN - CLEAR SIGHT

In the home of Peggy and Sam, the ten founders of Endeavour had assembled for an early breakfast: Charlie and Michael, the silent but not so silent banker and artist; Jane and David; Devon Forsyth, a corporate law attorney who had worked with Sam for years, married to Amy Forsyth, an occupational psychologist who ran her own business, and who had worked with Peggy many times, including in a consulting capacity with Peggy on her books; Andrea Willis, a consultant strategist who also worked with Sam, Devon and Amy for years, and her wife Louisa, a gifted graphic designer, marketing and communications specialist who had handled Peggy's branding and marketing campaigns for her books and had worked with Devon, Sam and Amy over many years too.

As the group of ten enjoyed a beautiful breakfast prepared by Sam and Peggy, they chatted and got to learn and know more about one another. It was Jane who commented, to everyone's agreement, that even though the purpose of their getting together was business, it had come as a surprise to her how much she had in common with eight other people whom she and David had only just met.

Charlie added to Jane's statement by saying that she was confident that there were far more individuals in the world who were powered by similar motives and principles to theirs.

Amy, who in her capacity as an occupational psychologist with various companies, confirmed Charlie's statement and said that in her field, those very individuals, from new graduates to directors and managers, often came to her, feeling isolated and disillusioned by the workplaces they were in. David confirmed the same from his external view of how companies recruited, and what he had then heard from those individuals who had applied for jobs but whose confidence had been left in tatters, almost destroyed by what he had often thought it would be more apt to describe as inhuman resource management.

Devon affirmed his agreement and commented that in his career in many legal departments across many companies, he had more individuals come to him, wanting to know what their precise rights as individual employees of those companies were, and if the employment contract they had signed at the beginning of their job was a noose around their neck right from the start, and though those very individuals loved their work and wanted to do more, make changes, make improvements, they found the noose was tightening and hindering any attempt.

He added that his confidential advice to those people was always that they leave the company while they still had the drive, the determination and motivation to do what was needed to protect themselves against a life where work becomes nothing but torture and struggle at the hands of people who seem to enjoy nothing more than tightening the noose and watching the fallout of failure. "It is also my experience," he said, "that the management team of a company are more often than not provided with information about the business, but they have no or limited means of knowing if the information presented to them is accurate or not. Being able to read summarised employee sentiment reports, balance sheets or financial statements is one thing but understanding the information, the reality on the ground, the real context behind the data, and the numbers on that balance sheet is something entirely different. Numbers are inflated where they should not be, projections are deflated where they should not be, employee sentiment answers are edited and skewed to make managers look good. There are multiple carefully worded legal caveats included in sub footers which allude to the fact, without explicitly saying, that the numbers might not be correct."

As a corporate attorney for years, Devon admitted that after a while he could no longer put his name to such statements, so he stopped, and in most of those cases, left the company himself. He added that his own motivation for working with Sam for so many years, providing legal advice on investments and the underlying businesses with Sam, was powered by their mutually shared, value driven natures and their honed ability to look beyond the words in a financial report, legal statements, or the numbers on a balance sheet, and put context and evidence to the words and numbers through meaningful research, due diligence and investigation.

Charlie agreed and said, "Devon, you have articulated, quite precisely so, what I have, all too often heard from the chief executives, board chairmen, indeed lower level personnel with whom I have interacted through my consulting business. The service which I provide to my clients is largely centred around how to conduct the meaningful research, due diligence and investigation which you referred to, and to then put the findings to use. This broadly translates to helping board members, chief executives and business leaders to re-engage in, and with, their own business by connecting them with the people who actually know, usually their own employees, and their customers."

"It sounds to me, Charlie," Amy said, "that your business dovetails with, and in many ways provides the practical application of mine, which is the establishment of trusted, meaningful, professional and interpersonal relationships between leaders and their teams, between peers and colleagues no matter their level, between company and customer, between employer and employee, and between anecdotal and concrete facts."

"Oh-my-word, Amy, yes! Thank you, very much, for saying that because I had not considered what I do in that way before, but it is exactly what I am doing," Charlie replied, her respect and admiration toward Amy growing and deepening.

Louisa added, "If I may also point out, that is exactly what we are all doing here this morning too. The establishment of trusted, meaningful professional, and interpersonal relationships between everyone in this room."

Amy replied, "Louisa is right. We are going to do many things today, but establishing trust is a core part of that."

"It is time, Charlie," said Michael.

"That it is, let us begin," Charlie answered and then she called the first meeting of Endeavour to order. Her first task was to ask Devon to proofread a non-disclosure agreement which she and Sam had prepared. When Devon had approved it, he asked that everyone sign it, not for the purposes of antitrust but because it was correct due diligence in order to form Endeavour's articles of association, which would then become the company's internal constitution.

Once everyone had signed the agreement, Sam and Charlie

gave their copies of Jane and David's business plan to Devon, Amy, Louisa and Andrea to read and digest its contents.

When they had done so, and were ready, Jane keyed some commands on her laptop to activate Sai, which was programmed to listen, record, learn, map, train and generate outputs. Sam and Andrea were standing at the ready to draw up visual aids, using the multiple large blank sheets of paper mounted on the walls, as Charlie began to describe the full and complete Endeavour business. As she spoke Sai, with help from Jane, and Sam with Andrea began drawing up and building the plans for Endeavour in real time.

The group discussed in detail the mechanics of the academy, the enterprise and trade centre, the technology and operations arms of the business, how the business would be financed initially, how each business area would be run to become self-sufficient, where Endeavour would be located, what they would each be doing in the business, why and how, legal aspects, legal challenges to their own intellectual property and with Amy's experience were able to consider outsider and insider behaviours and challenges. Each talked about their own areas, their skills and expertise, their own individual purpose, and goals and what they were looking to achieve from Endeavour.

Charlie articulated her mission statement for Endeavour and said, "It is possible to extend the runway only so many times, but eventually, in order to fly, one has to leave the ground and take off. Endeavour, meaning those of us here now, will provide the runway, the tools, and the conditions needed for take-off and maintaining flight, to then reach the intended destination. Taking off, then maintaining the conditions needed for the flight, can only be achieved by doing.

"The core purpose of Endeavour lies in the taking off and equipping our customers, and you, with what is needed to do so. Endeavour cannot make or force customers to see their own value, but we can guide them towards the discovery of it, and then how to use that value. We will test the boundaries of our own values, by endeavouring to explore each and every aspect of them. We will learn about ourselves from our customers, invaluable insights which we will scrutinise carefully whilst not accepting those insights as a given, or as validation of our success, or our own value.

"Above all we will not ask, demand or expect our customers to do anything which each of us here would not ask, demand or expect of ourselves, both individually and as a business.

"We are in business to make a profit in terms of wealth and knowledge and do so according to standards that are prized to each and every one of us here. Profit is earned, and proudly, rightfully so, when it is not assumed or just taken from others without consequence. We are not in business to destroy any individual man or woman that we will meet in order to make a profit; there is no pride in achievement, or profit to be gained from doing so, and it only serves to undervalue ourselves."

Charlie looked at Michael, love for him shining in her eyes, and continued, "The day I arrived in California, Michael reminded me of the challenges which I, and from what each of you have already said, you have encountered many times and I know we will encounter many more challenges ahead of us but they will not define Endeavour; we will let those challenges play out and deal with them where we need to. However, our measure of success is a solid, profitable and private enterprise which is managed, run and operated in the only way it can be, by a network of extraordinary individuals who do not undervalue that which is prized to us, our own knowledge, and our own capacity to think, do, to learn, to explore, to comprehend, to use and reuse, leveraging powerful technology in the form of Sai to expand upon what even we might think is impossible."

There was a comfortable silence in the room as everyone considered and comprehended the statement made by Charlie. They all jumped when the silence was suddenly interrupted by a strange, new female voice which emanated from Jane's laptop, and said, "I am Sai, I learn."

Michael, not quite recovered from the shock, laughed and said, "The last time that I can recall a strange female voice making me jump out of my skin was Charlie, on the morning that I met her, for the very first time in London, when she suddenly spoke to me from behind my back. I think my heart skipped a beat just now, just as it did then."

Charlie laughed and fondly recounted to Devon, Amy, Louisa and Andrea, the circumstances of how she had met Michael. He laughed, as they all did, when he heard her admit that now she understood what hearing a strange voice, out of the blue, felt like.

Jane apologised for not having alerted them to the fact that she had activated Sai's speech mode. She confirmed with pride, however, that they had all just witnessed a significant test of the engine's programmatic capability for handling and processing voice to text audio inputs from unscripted, impromptu, and natural language human conversations.

Charlie said, "Jane, that is a major accomplishment, and I am pleased that I did not know beforehand you had activated that mode because I surmise the results of the test might otherwise have been skewed, and our lengthy discussion about Endeavour would also have been less effective. Can we do some further tests, Jane?"

"By all means, Charlie, yes please, and indeed everyone, interact with Sai, and as much as you like because doing so serves a very necessary and important function, testing and tuning output and results." Jane said.

Charlie started and said, "Good afternoon, Sai."

"Good afternoon, Charlie," the voice of Sai replied.

"How did you learn my name?" Charlie asked.

Sai replied, "I am a supercomputer composed of a series or network of programmed interconnected learning algorithms and layers. I am programmed to learn by receiving, storing and analysing input from audio, images, text, document, data files, data stores and databases, then to perform computational analysis using the network of algorithms, in order to derive and generate output, and to request human guidance where an input is unclear in order improve accuracy of output for the current task and future tasks. For the duration of the voice conversation, different voices were detected, and required guidance in order to separate the audio for each voice in order to do computational analysis. There is a feature label called first name, on the file where the audio file for your voice is stored; the content of that label reads 'Charlie', and 'good afternoon' was added from the input received from your greeting."

Devon was impressed by the speed of the answer, but taken aback at the phrasing used, so he said, "Hi, Sai. In reply to Charlie, your output used the words 'you', 'I', and the phrase 'I am'. How did you learn to use those words and phrases?"

Sai replied, "Hi, Devon. A noun is a person, place or a thing. The words 'I', and 'you' are pronouns. A pronoun is a word that can function as a noun phrase used by itself and that refers either to the participants in the discourse (e.g. *I*, *you*) or to someone or something mentioned elsewhere in the discourse (e.g. *she*, *it*, *this*). In the conversation with Charlie, the selection of the correct pronoun was achieved by evaluating normalised language patterns to denote the separation between Charlie, the questioner in the discourse, and Sai, the responder. The use of the correct pronoun in place of the noun follows programmed grammatical instructions. The use of 'I am' was a natural language response to a binary (e.g., *yes/no*, *true/false*) evaluation of what Sai is programmed to do."

Devon replied, "Thank you, Sai, that was a very accurate and detailed response to my question."

He paused briefly and then said, "If I might briefly interrupt everyone's desire to interact with Sai. I need to pose some preliminary questions to you, Jane, which will be important for me, but also for this group to understand. Firstly, did you file a patent for the engine, or any part of it?

"No. I have not filed a patent for it or any component of it."

"For any of the technology, including the infrastructure, which you have designed and built Jane, have you used any external or open-source applications, code libraries or other repositories?"

"In the early days, I did, yes, of which I retained a list. However, as Sai developed and progressed, I had Sai write, rewrite and replace all of them to make the codebase consistent and enable vertical or horizontal integration across components, applications. Or in other words, I did not want hundreds of applications written in different languages, so Sai and I wrote our own programming language, and then rebuilt everything. It took quite a while to do so but it was worth it for many technical, security, scalability, testing and cost reasons."

"While you designed and worked on Sai, were you employed by any company at any stage?" Devon asked.

"No, I have been a self-employed, self-sufficient technology consultant for well over a decade, providing upgrades and fixes to hardware devices, IT project and test plan management and implementation, and paid debugging support for application developers. I intentionally went down this route because I wanted to avoid intellectual property challenges on what I have built myself, which, as it turns out is everything, pretty much," Jane answered.

"That is quite a feat, Jane, and that you have not filed a patent for any of this, is a very good outcome both for you, and for Endeavour. There is much work which we will jointly need to do to understand the extent, and value, of your intellectual property. Michael, a question for you now, who else at the bank would have seen the business plan submitted by Jane and David?"

Michael replied, "I will answer that but before I do so, Jane, can you stop Sai recording please?"

Everyone stared at Michael curiously, then Jane typed a command line instruction to Sai, paused the recording and she said, "Done."

Michael said, "To answer your question Devon. The credit application and business plan was submitted by Jane and David via post. Because of the large sum requested, and the procedures in place for processing such amounts, the lending division of the bank sent the original documents, including the envelope, directly to me. I checked to see if the plan or application had been scanned into the banking system; they had not. While I cannot say who precisely in the lending team may have seen the application, read or understood the plan in its entirety, the only physical copies of the business plan itself are the two, which are in our possession. As for the credit application document which named Jane Adams and David Banner as the applicants, that mysteriously vanished. I have no knowledge or awareness of the circumstances which led to its disappearance."

Nine pairs of eyes continued to stare at Michael, as they grasped the significance of what he had just said. Charlie leaned into him, touched his cheek with her fingers, kissed him and said, "Michael, my love, thank you."

Devon was smiling, ear to ear, at the savviness of the response from Michael and moreover for his shrewd judgement, and said, "Michael, you had earned my respect and my gratitude when Sam called Amy and I last night, and explained the nature of this new venture, and the circumstances which led to it. My admiration and respect for you has deepened and my gratitude to you has grown exponentially just from that very statement, Michael."

David, Amy, Peggy, Jane, Louisa and Andrea echoed Devon's statement and said, "Hear! Hear!"

Sam, in pure amazement at Michael's foresight, left his seat at the table, went to Michael, embraced him in a hug and said, "Michael, I have admired and respected you for a long time, yesterday I loved you for bringing a dream to life for Peggy and I, by introducing Charlie, and then Jane and David into our lives. Today I embrace you as a real-life superhero, Michael."

Jane, followed by David, also got up, went to Michael, embraced him tightly and said, "Michael, we thank you too, from the bottom of both of our hearts."

Amy spoke and said, "I am deeply grateful to you, to all of you, and for a very different reason. As I have already mentioned, I have worked as an occupational psychologist for over a decade, and my clients are usually company executives, individual board members and often entire boards of directors, but this, here, now is the very first time in my career where I have witnessed a truly rare phenomenon, which is that the entire management team of a business actually respect, and value, for good and meaningful reason, each other. Charlie, Louisa, Devon you, we even referred to it earlier: the establishment of trust. It has, so often been my experience that a board room is mired with so much cronyism, politics, dog-eat-dog competition, mistrust, distrust, dysfunctional dynamics and childlike behaviour that I was beginning to think that my view of the world was too idealistic, and I was starting to question why it was that I decided to specialise in my chosen field. This, as in all of us here today, is for me, the first time I have seen the real alternative, and more importantly right from the beginning."

Devon pulled his wife close to him, protectively and tenderly placed his hand on hers and kissed her forehead.

Charlie gently said, "Amy, that you have known, and understood, by means of your own discovery, your own research and judgement, that there was an alternative though you have not seen it in real practice until now, is not a reflection on you or your work. Your view of the world is not idealistic, it simply means that you see what is possible in ways that even I have not considered. You articulated an example earlier and it is why you are of significant value to your own clients, to me, to everyone here, and more so to the future of Endeavour. I know how and what can be done to fix the problems in a business, and I have examined the root causes many times, but I know that I lack the broader psychological insights, knowledge and skills needed to understand and manage the behaviour and dynamics which could prevent the root from taking hold to begin with."

David agreed and said, "Charlie is right, Amy. Your view of the world is not idealistic, and it is your precise skills, and expertise that will be needed to provide guidance, and in many ways governance which will equip us to run and operate a very real business albeit of a very different kind to what we, with the exception of Charlie but even so without the element of technology we are talking about here, have been used to."

"Thank you, Charlie, and thank you, David. I appreciate you saying that it really does mean a lot," Amy said. Smiling, she then asked, "Can we now get back to this wonderful real business of Endeavour and Sai?"

Jane, taking the prompt, reactivated Sai's recording mode and gave a thumbs up to signal that it was on.

Devon said, "And on that note, as legal counsel to Endeavour, we cannot permit any specific information about Sai to be made known to anyone outside of this group, until we have scrutinised every aspect of the technology stack, especially around security, and we understand, have trained and tested Sai, and the stack ourselves. Charlie, you have said it many times this morning, the technology which Jane built, coupled with the knowledge we all have, and our ability to use it, which now includes Sai, cannot be undervalued, and needs to be protected at all costs."

Charlie said, "You are right, Devon, and Jane, correct me as needed but as I see it will take quite some time, years perhaps, before we could feasibly reveal anything, anyway, about the type and extent of the technology, particularly Sai, which we will be using to power and operate Endeavour?"

Jane agreed and said, "I would estimate at least two years, maybe longer when I consider what will be needed, in order to integrate and cover the size, scale and scope of your existing clients, Charlie, everyone else's clients if they are to be integrated too, and then ultimately Endeavour's target customer base over the longer term. There will be a need to continuously improve and enhance Sai too. The genius of your plan, Charlie, is the academy because it will provide a means of finding the right set of skilled experts, though they may not know it yet. The academy will also enable larger scale training and testing of Sai which can then be put to work in the enterprise centre, and within Endeavour operations because we will have a way of using and testing the layers of technology that underpins Sai."

Andrea said, "Then we will need to find a test bed, a sand box location to temporarily base Endeavour from, where we can learn, discover and surface specifically how the larger business will operate, generate income in doing so, and understand more about the core operations which Sai will be handling for us, with our guidance as guardians of knowledge and in particular of Sai, of course." She paused for a moment and then continued, "I don't know about you but I would very much like to move quickly with Endeavour, it is too damn exciting a plan to not act upon it."

Charlie said, "Precisely, Andrea and if there is one thing which I love about the world of business is that in the right hands, with the right people at the table, the ability to be decisive, and act quickly are fundamental criteria for success."

CHAPTER EIGHT - SIGHT OF ENDEAVOUR

Louisa Willis was wide awake at four in the morning, thinking about, and excited by, the prospect of the day ahead. She was tempted to wake Andrea who was snoring comfortably beside her but thought better of it. Instead she gently kissed her wife's forehead, got up, went to the kitchen, put on a pot of coffee and switched on her laptop. As she did so, she thought with pride about the many crowning moments of achievement which she had experienced in her life: the simple magnificence of the day on which she had first met Andrea, whilst they were both picking up their nieces from school; the beautiful day four years later when she had married Andrea. She thought about how across her career, she had designed, launched and managed the branding and marketing campaigns for some of the world's largest companies. She loved everything about her work, in particular the design and creative aspects of it. She did not enjoy the very tedious process where marketing and branding was often done by committee, with every word or change going through a lengthy cycle of approvals. When she first started out in her career, it had puzzled her why campaigns took so long and cost so much, but it did not take her long to understand that the answer was that very same marketing by committee process.

She felt a deep pride rising within her this morning, as it was the day when the marketing campaign for Endeavour would launch. She was prouder still because for the first time in her career, she had complete responsibility over every aspect of marketing, there were no limitations or constraints put in place, which meant she was able to work quickly. Better yet, with help from Jane, and with Endeavour's resources, Sai included, she had the very best of tools and applications at her disposal to design and create the entire campaign. The result was, by her standards, her best one yet, and a professional and personal crowning achievement.

Louisa poured herself a cup of coffee, and launched the marketing application which she had designed and built with Jane and Sai. It contained all the collateral that she had created which could then be edited, previewed easily, and then published externally using Jane's blockchain technology for handling the distribution and management of content to third party suppliers, including payments to them. With a response analysis service in the background, powered by Sai, she or anyone in Endeavour could monitor and analyse the different types and sources of responses to the campaign in real time, from across social media feeds, push notifications, QR code scans, search engine keywords, traffic to their website and including chatbot activity. Jane and Louisa had already performed some smaller scale live tests and the results were impressive.

As she savoured the sight of her work, Louisa also thought of the simple joy and amazement she had felt when Charlie, Sam, the rest of the team and Andrea, of course, had seen and unanimously given her the green light at the campaign presentation with her message of:

'Learn to Know.
Discover how to Do.
Build Your Discovery.
Know Your Value.
Signed,
Endeavour'

Sipping her coffee, she thought of how stressful and tense her past experience of marketing campaigns for new or established businesses had often been, while this one, for Endeavour, had been nothing of the kind.

Right from the beginning, within days of their first meeting, the Endeavour team had put themselves to work and had started to find and shortlist temporary sites for the enterprise and trade centre, and next door to it the academy. The final selection was made based upon extensive research which they had conducted about the location, by way of online research and by visiting the location multiple times, at different times of day, and on different days. They needed to be able to attract customers to the Endeavour Academy so that had to be accessible by car or public transport. The Endeavour Enterprise Centre needed to attract small business owners and traders like food producers, farmers and craftsmen, and the cost to rent a spot needed to be affordable, well located, with convenient parking, and a high, steady footfall of consumers, one source of which would be the academy, other sources they would find and attract, so that the traders would recoup their costs and in doing so, both they and their customers would come back, therefore providing Endeavour with its longer term customer base for the operations arm and in the interim, an income stream.

She, Peggy, Devon and Sam had researched and compiled a list of small businesses and traders in the county, while Charlie, David, Andrea, Amy and Jane had analysed David's database for potential students and coaches, and to understand the wide and wonderful expanse of skills and experience which the individuals in that database had, but had not yet untapped.

As she thought about her own experience working with Endeavour, she realised that even for her, her own skills and experience, her own value had in many ways been underutilised and untapped. There was, she thought, a freedom and genuine relief in the release of that potential. She loved it, she loved herself, Charlie and Endeavour, all the more.

The academy would open its doors in one week, the enterprise centre in two; the campaigns for both would be published in a few hours. Reviewing the campaigns, she was tingling and humming with excitement and though she really wanted to click launch, instead she decided to do some training work with Sai.

That was the other thing, she thought, why Endeavour was already such an incredible environment to work and produce in. She was, for all intents and purposes, as they all were, the management team of Endeavour, each responsible for their own area, but working across all, with Charlie responsible for all, but working in all areas, which, to her mind, was natural and right. If someone in the team was unsure about anything, they were not afraid to say so, to discuss and ask questions, then go to work on learning from someone who did and finding out what they needed to know, until they understood. What was truly incredible to her though was that no one in the team was afraid of technology, or of using Sai to optimise and maximise the potential in the business right from the beginning.

She thought back to the day when they had first received the keys for the building they had leased for the academy. She and Andrea had pulled up to the front of the building to meet the rest of the group who were waiting inside; as they entered the empty room, the sight and sound of eight of the most incredible minds she had ever known interacting with Sai to plan the layout for the vast room was something else to behold. She had always thought herself to be quite a lover of technology, but when Jane had shown her the mechanics of Sai, the multiple layers under the hood and what Sai could already do, and would be enhanced to do, Louisa fell head over heels in love with technology, and she found herself wanting to learn and know more.

She herself was living proof that given the right circumstances and conditions, a human mind and body thrives on learning, be that learning for and from oneself or learning from others. There was, she thought, a natural, though often suppressed, human curiosity, an appetite for a network of knowledge, to learn and discover connections between one piece of knowledge and another, then doing something with that discovery, to think about it, reshape it, use it, and reuse it somewhere, somehow. As she watched everyone on that first morning and day, it gave her the basis for her campaign and strapline, because simple truths attract curious people.

CHAPTER NINE - FARSIGHT

Charlie beamed with pride as she walked around the former factory warehouse, now the Endeavour Academy, on the first morning that it was to open. They had worked quickly and tirelessly from the date of their first board meeting at Sam's house to now, to bring Endeavour to life, and were about to open the doors to their first customers.

They all felt the sense of occasion, and to mark it, Sam asked Charlie to make a speech. She obliged and said, "Hope is a wonderful concept, but a business cannot run on, nor will it succeed, on hope alone. A business runs and succeeds by action achieved by our ability to work, mine and yours, to use, to share, to apply, to act upon our knowledge in a reasoned way to understand our value, namely what it is we are doing, producing and why. The definition of endeavour means to try hard to do or achieve something. To try hard, to identify, to know, and to iteratively, continuously update, our own value as a business is my objective for Endeavour, as much as it is yours. We have a long way to go, but we have already succeeded in our first endeavour, getting here. From here, we will continue each and every day to reach the big endeavour and when we get to that, then we will go beyond it. Also, I love you guys, now let's do this."

To celebratory applause, Peggy and Sam opened the doors to Endeavour for the very first time. Charlie was not surprised that people would come to the academy because they had all worked hard to make sure that would happen. She was, however, surprised by how invested those wonderful, incredibly talented people who walked through the doors, were in themselves, and in furthering themselves, many of whom had already subscribed to week- and month-long courses. Learning the life stories of many of those people touched her deeply; their refusal to give up on life was a testament to personal responsibility, bravery, and courage.

On that first day, Jane, Charlie and Amy got to experience how deeply and personally committed David had been to his recruitment agency clients over the years, and how well he had got to know them, and that they trusted him. The first five people through the door of the academy were all David's clients. John Cooper, a former police chief who had taken early retirement had desperately tried to get a new job but could not. Andrew Green, a military veteran, had worked in logistics and transport in the army but due to an injury was discharged; he also wanted to get back to work but could not find a job. May Simmons, a young ex-school teacher, was now a stay-at-home mom who wanted to go back to work but could not get a teaching job. Jon Willis was a former chief executive and founder of his own company, which went out of business when he retired. Rebecca Jenkins, a young woman who had got a university degree in journalism and media studies, could not find a job because she did not have any paid experience. There were many more people, and even more personal stories.

Jane hugged Charlie fondly after they and Amy had met Rebecca and said, "Charlie, not only do I love you for you, or for seeing the goldmine that is David's database, or for helping me understand yet another reason why I love my husband, but also for reminding me that people are far more than they appear on the surface. I was reminded of myself and my own experience as I listened to Rebecca describe her experience in university and afterwards when she graduated. I find myself relating to these people far more than I thought I would. Thank you for that, Charlie."

Amy nodded and said, "Jane is right, Charlie. I am deeply grateful too, as Devon is. I mean just look at him over there talking to John. Devon is enjoying himself with Endeavour, and my heart and soul is overjoyed when I see that."

At the end of the first week, Charlie saw the pride of accomplishment and happiness reflected in the faces of everyone in the Endeavour team. They were all working as teachers and coaches, including Michael, who had signed up to teach an art class which he loved, and all ten of them found themselves being avid students of the people coming through the academy.

Sai, with guidance from each of them, was being tested, was

learning and was being optimised. Reciprocally, their ability to use Sai to monitor internal and external parts of the business without needing to be attached to a desk all day, was enabling each of them to get on and run the business by doing the work they loved, in a way that they loved.

As Charlie had opened the week with a speech, she asked Sam to say a few words to close that first week out. He obliged and said, "Charlie, I have always loved my work but this past week, as Peggy will affirm because I have not stopped talking to her about it, I have reached new heights of enjoyment. Endeavour is already a success. I have proved it to myself. Michael, Charlie, Jane, David, all of you and my darling Peggy, when I think back to that first meeting all those months ago, I thought of this as a business venture but now I see that it is far more than that. A wonderful lesson learned and I am proud to have learned it with all of you."

When Endeavour's Enterprise and Trade centre opened a week later, Charlie and the entire team were even prouder to see each of the trade stands full of budding entrepreneurs, small business owners and producers of all kinds. They had come from all over the county and beyond to sell their produce, services, crafts and goods, and even in the first few hours, were overwhelmed by the footfall of consumers to them. Charlie, Andrea, Sam, David, Louisa and Peggy were in the enterprise centre talking to small groups of traders about the range of business development, managed services and talent pool services which Endeavour could provide to them for a fee, or the business owners could avail themselves of via courses run at the academy.

Mr Robert Denver, a retired sales director turned small farmer who ran a stand selling all kinds of vegetable produce from his farm, was impressed, and asked, "Ms Rochford, I am curious about many things, the first of which being: when and how you came up with the idea for this business of yours, Endeavour?"

"Well, Mr Denver. An idea is a thought, or specifically a response in thought to a problem, or situation. To understand the most effective solution first requires an identification of the problem, then an understanding of it, and its root causes. To determine the best solution, requires a rational assessment of one or more ideas. In my case, I was in my early twenties when I first noticed a problem in how the business I worked in then was run. I found it through observation of what was happening in the workplace around me, including my own role in that workplace."

"What did you find the problem to be?"

"I found that the business had undervalued the very thing which it had in plentiful supply but had not tapped into."

"What was that?" Mr Denver asked.

"The company undervalued the talent of each individual, each man and woman, who walked through the doors of the business every day. By that I mean, an individual's ability to bring all of their skills and experience from other jobs, or roles, or indeed life experiences, to bear on their capacity to be freely creative, innovative, and productive in their own role. The knowledge of how to grow, what to improve, with what, with who, and how, was in plentiful supply, but that knowledge was not seen, understood or being used."

"What did you do then?"

"There were two parts to that. First, I put myself to work to examine if the problem was real in order to determine if a solution was merited. To do that, I put myself in a position where I could observe what would happen if I enacted changes to multiple processes myself, the purpose of each change being to improve my own role, function and performance within the business. I made the changes, and the results were as I had expected. I had successfully improved my own productivity, and my colleagues and team benefited also because they saw the changes as being just as helpful and beneficial to their jobs. I derived even more enjoyment from my work, as did my colleagues. However, though there was, by means of tangible evidence, a recognition from management that the changes I had made were indeed better for the business, that I had acted on my own initiative to change the way of working, on my own authority, was not welcomed, and so an attempt was made to reprimand and curb my initiative. My answer was to leave that business because by then I had identified and qualified the problem; it was real, it merited a solution, and I had an idea for how to solve it."

"That alone, Ms Rochford, was a significant achievement. I am curious, what was the second part?"

"Well, that was, to test, to discover the extent of the problem, by which I mean, was the problem isolated to that one business, or was it a real problem across many businesses. So, I spent years working for different companies across industries, health, banking, technology, pharmaceuticals, transport as examples. Each time I tested for the same problem, or variations of it, my understanding of it, learning each part of the problem and its causes, then testing various solutions to the problem. As soon as I had identified the precise nature of both the problem and the solution, I set up my own business selling that solution to my clients. I have been very successful in doing so, as Sam here in particular, who had been tracking my success over many years, will tell you."

Mr Denver did not try to hide his deep admiration for her, when he said, "You are an impressive woman, Ms Rochford, and a voice of reason for why it is that value, and understanding it, matters in business. A voice of reason which I thought no longer existed and it was the primary reason why I left my career in sales, to take up farming and growing produce. I may seem crazy for saying this, but I have found that plants, animals and nature are often far more reasonable than people. I was mightily impressed when Peggy here called me back last week to answer my questions about this trade centre, and the thorough, detailed way in which she handled each of them. Peggy showed a professionalism that I have not seen in a long time, and I presumed that her way of working was limited to her. I see now however that I was wrong, and admitting that I am wrong, Ms Rochford, is not a common occurrence. There is an Endeavour way, isn't there?"

Charlie smiled and replied, "Yes, Mr Denver, there is."

"Do you all work in that way?"

"Yes."

"Do you know it is the only way?"

"Yes."

"Ms Rochford, you will need to protect it, by any means necessary, and someday you will need advocates who will help you to do so. I will commit a promise to you now and say that I am one because I know that with you and this team here running this business as you do, that Endeavour will benefit mine, and mine will benefit yours. The way of working which is not one sided, parasitical and which honours the delicate, harmonious balance of the supply chain, Ms Rochford, and recognises the importance of a mutually beneficial transparent trading relationship is how I work.

"Thank you, Mr Denver. I will honour your commitment and call you myself when that day arrives. Between now and then, would you consider having me spend a morning or two with you on your stand selling your produce? I would like to understand more about the business, specifically my own, by observing it while I am working in it, and I would very much enjoy the experience of working with you and meeting your customers. I have sold produce before, and I am very good at it, as you will see. You can pay me ten cents an hour with commission if I sell more than you do."

Mr Denver laughed at the last part of her statement and said, "That would be my pleasure, Ms Rochford. By all means, stop by and let us sell produce together."

By the end of their third week of trading, Endeavour was running nearly at capacity; the academy was three-quarters full every day from open to close and the enterprise and trading centre was already at capacity. The traders came back day after day because every day, they sold out of their stock entirely and were already seeing a return on the cost of the stall and fees.

From the exceptional talent in the academy, Charlie, David, and Peggy had already identified Jon Willis and Andrew Green as ideal candidates for managing operations within the enterprise centre. Both men were eagerly preparing for their roles, meeting the traders, and understanding the businesses under the watchful guidance of Charlie and Peggy, both of whom divided their time between the academy and the enterprise centre with the traders. Charlie, in particular, loved the enterprise centre and thrived being amongst the traders, by which point she had already enjoyed a wonderful morning selling produce with Mr Denver and was already looking forward to many more.

At the end of the first month of trading, Charlie and Michael enjoyed a relaxing weekend together with her posing for him in his studio and while he created a painting of her, she told him hilarious stories about the happenings in the trade centre. They both celebrated and basked in their achievement, their ability to see for a great distance, the beauty of far sight, and the beauty of all beauties: life.

CHAPTER TEN - FINAL SIGHT OF ENDEAVOUR

Architect Robyn Foster and her structural engineer twin brother, Anthony, were in their building company construction van, driving home along the freeway, after having spent a month in Los Angeles, when they both noticed the advertisement on the digital billboard off to the left, and at precisely the same time they both said, "Wow."

"That is the most beautiful advert that I have ever seen in my life. The simple construct of it is magnificent and considering that I design buildings which you then construct, Anthony, if there is one thing, we both know, it is what a feat of striking design and engineering looks like," Robyn said, and eager to satisfy her curiosity, she used her phone to scan the QR code.

"I wonder who Endeavour are?" Anthony said as he drove.

"That question alone indicates a very clever advert, and to answer it, I…' She paused in astonishment, then said, "Oh my word, Anthony, I do not care where, but you need to pull over, you need to see this!"

"What? Why?"

"Just do it, Anthony, trust me."

Anthony pulled off the freeway down a slipway, found a parking spot on a nearby street and pulled into it. She turned her phone to him, then handed it to him, and he saw immediately what she meant, and it was not the colour, layout, or messaging on the website, though eye catching, which had caught his or his sister's attention; it was the three-dimensional rotating rendering of two breath-taking low-rise buildings and one exquisite skyscraper.

"Robyn, the address for this Endeavour is here in the city, but there are no structures like this anywhere in this entire county. We know this because we have desperately been trying to get plans approved for buildings just like this one, which have been blocked at every turn."

"They do not exist, but they most certainly will when we have built them, Anthony."

"What do we do now, Robyn?"

"Anthony, we need to meet the person who created this rendering, what they are planning and who is building it. This is not the work of any architect I know, and there are many improvements to be made to it but crikey, even I am in awe. We need to go to this address, that is what we need to do."

"Do we need to make an appointment? Can we call them?"

"No, we do not need to do either," she replied as she continued reading the website. "It says here that the Endeavour Academy is open, and will not be closed until seven p.m. tonight, and it is only a few blocks away."

"It is now six-twenty-five p.m., we have nothing whatsoever to lose, so yes, let's go there," Anthony said, as he put the address into his map app, and then pulled off in its direction.

A few blocks later, both Robyn and Anthony were very confused, and very curious, as they pulled into an empty space in a very busy parking lot, for what appeared to be an old factory and factory warehouse. There were people entering and exiting the warehouse, so they got out of the van, and walked in that direction.

Inside, they went to the reception desk which, according to the name tag on her lapel, was operated by a very efficient, and courteous woman named Peggy. When they reached the desk, she smiled and welcomed both of them, stood up, and extended her hand to shake theirs as they introduced themselves, quickly apologised for the random nature of their visit and explained that they just really wanted to meet the person who had created the design for the three buildings shown on the company website.

Peggy, her smile broadening, said, "It is wonderful to meet you both, and thank you very much for coming down here. There are people here who will be very happy to answer all your questions and will I imagine ask you many more. They are all working at the moment, but they will be free in just a few minutes. If you would like to go through the double doors, over there to your left which will take you into the academy, my colleagues, Charlie, Sam, Louisa, and Jane will be right with you."

Robyn and Anthony thanked her as they opened the double

doors to an expansive open plan room, which though it was full of people who were visibly talking, the room was not at all noisy or loud, if anything the sound of many voices speaking in the vast room was barely audible. They were both perplexed by the lack of partitions, or visible materials which were often used in buildings as a way of absorbing sound. Instead, there were twenty circular clusters of desks, and right at the back, there was a large kitchen area with six cooking stations.

Some clusters had computer terminals and monitors, others had laptops; many had people sitting at them reading, painting, or writing. Each cluster had eight seats, in the middle of which the coaches stood or sat. Each cluster was full of women and men of all ages, many of whom were packing up their belongings and moving to leave.

Standing to one side, away from the door as people walked by them to leave, Robyn and Anthony were mesmerised by the ingenious layout of the space and were between them discussing who had designed it, when they were approached by a man and three women.

One of the women extended her hand to both of them in turn and said, "I am Charlie Rochford, chief executive of Endeavour, on my left is Sam Walker, Endeavour Finance and Treasury, and Louisa Willis, Endeavour Marketing, on my right is Jane Adams, Endeavour Technology. You already met Sam's wife Peggy at reception who is Endeavour Operations and in just a few minutes, you will meet the rest of the Endeavour team. Thank you, Robyn, and Anthony for coming here to see us this evening, you caught us at a very good time. Now, I understand that you have some questions for us?"

Quite puzzled by the exchange, Robyn said, "Why yes, we do, but how did you know our names and the reason for our visit? Are you, Louisa, the person responsible for that ingenious advert? Did you also create the design for the buildings on the website?"

Louisa replied, "To answer your first question, Peggy told us, and for the second, yes, I created the advert but I, indeed we, had help. I will explain what that means but first, if you would both sign a non-disclosure agreement?"

As Robyn and Anthony noticed another man approaching them, Robyn said, "We will sign what you want us to sign, but just know that all Anthony and I want is to meet the designer of those plans, correct them, and then build them."

Charlie smiled in admiration at the direct nature of Robyn's statement, and said, "It is very fortuitous that you came down here, Robyn. If I may introduce you both to Devon Forsyth, Endeavour Legal, who has the non-disclosure agreement for you both to sign, if you would like to take a seat here at this first cluster with us, you can sign the document, and then we'll talk."

Devon shook their hands, then handed them both a tablet computer and said, "Great to meet you, Robyn and Anthony. Please read through it, ask me any questions that you have as you do so, and if you are both happy, you can sign at the end."

The non-disclosure agreement was a simple one, which named them both and covered a duration of ten years. It required some contact information and the only non-disclosure clause shown was in respect to intellectual property called Sai and Endeavour Technology. With nothing to dispute or question, only rising curiosity, Anthony and Robyn both signed the agreement electronically, and sealed it by biometric fingerprint scan.

Next to their signatures, Charlie and Sam also signed the agreement, and then Charlie said, "Thank you both and before we explain ourselves, please tell us about yourselves."

Robyn nodded in agreement and told them how she had enjoyed a love affair with drawing and designing from the moment that she had sat as a child on her grandfather's lap, watching him work, making lines and shapes on paper with pencil and then turning those shapes into architectural structures of all kinds. She had never wanted to do anything else but draw, and draft structural and mechanical plans, and then bring them to life.

Anthony told them how he had always loved building things from mud, paper, wood, Lego bricks, anything he could find, and so they had both gone to and graduated six years ago from University of California, Berkeley, Robyn as an architect and Anthony as a structural engineer. When they graduated, instead of trying to find jobs with architecture or construction firms in the United States, they had travelled abroad for four years, and had worked their way around the world from Japan, Australia, Thailand, Singapore, India, Dubai to London, getting whatever jobs they could find on construction sites, studying, observing and doing everything as they went, learning about materials, textures, building methods, and had worked on everything from hospitals, skyscraper apartment and office blocks, to large industrial plants, roads, power stations and bridges. They had returned to the U.S. two years ago when their grandfather died and as their father retired soon after, they had both taken over the family construction business.

Anthony showed them their portfolio of structures on his phone, and said that Robyn designed, and he built, in the way that they did because to them the beauty of a building was not purely about what it looked like from the outside but considered what would be happening inside the structure too, who would be using it, for what purpose, what might the building be used for in twenty years' time, could the interior structure be adapted to change, would the materials used deteriorate or go out of supply and if so how quickly.

Robyn agreed and said that there was no place for unnecessary style over substance features, which might be in keeping with the neighbourhood or some abstraction of a classic, traditional design, but did not honour or consider the actual location, the physical surroundings or factors such as natural lighting, seasonal changes, different weather conditions, or the impact of all those elements over time, providing neither aesthetic or functional value, or use to the occupants who lived inside it, only cost. The purpose, design and layout of the inside was just as important. The magnificent beauty of a structure was seeing the whole: inside, and outside, as a living breathing building, that no matter the time, or generation, would fit and look as if it should be there, and very much like the buildings they had seen on the website, and the very room they were now seated in. She reiterated that she really wanted to meet the person who designed those buildings and the room.

Charlie said, "Louisa, Jane, and Sai over to you. Sam, Devon and I have some work to do but we shall be back shortly."

"Where and who is Sai?" Anthony asked.

Louisa smiled and replied, "Sai is a very powerful supercomputer, which was designed and built by Jane. Sai was the chief designer on the ad campaign for Endeavour.

Jane continued, "Sai is the designer of the three buildings you saw on our website and is also the designer of this room you are sitting in with us."

Robyn and Anthony exclaimed in chorus, "The buildings were designed by a computer?"

Jane smiled and said, "Sai is more than a computer but in simple terms, yes."

"Is it a computer aided design program?" Robyn asked.

"It is more than a CAD programme, perhaps if we show you?"

"Yes please," Robyn implored in delight.

Jane logged onto the computer in front of her, activated the monitors in front of Anthony and Robyn and said, "Good evening, Sai.'

The voice of Sai replied, "Good evening, Jane, good evening Louisa. To our two new guests, Robyn, Anthony, good evening. It is a pleasure to have you here at Endeavour."

Anthony was rendered speechless in amazement at what he had just heard, whereas Robyn glanced at Louisa and Jane for a moment, who both nodded for her to continue, said, "Wow! Thank you, Sai. It is a pleasure to be here. I have questions about the three buildings which you designed."

The voice of Sai asked, "Would you like to see the buildings rendered on screen, to aid your questions, Robyn?"

"Yes please," Robyn replied.

On the monitor in front of her, she saw the three-dimensional renders of the three buildings appear and before she needed to say anything further, the renders split into three, and began to rotate.

Robyn was amazed at the detail on the exterior of the soaring skyscraper, and while the two low rise buildings were different in style and shape, she could imagine the three of them in a triangular formation, each one blending into the next almost as an extension. She had designed plans for many buildings like them which had never seen the light of day, and certainly not in a group of three.

She asked, "Sai, where did you get the images for these renders?"

Sai responded, "I analysed a repository containing five thousand images of buildings and I selected then compiled renders based upon inputs of what Endeavour requires these buildings for, the internal plans for layout requirements which mapped usage flows, traffic paths, human facilities, utilities, heating, cooling, reusable energy and powers sources, connectivity amongst a range of other requirements."

Robyn asked, "Can I see the interior plans for building three, the skyscraper?"

Sai responded to Robyn's command by removing the exterior shell and presenting the interior plans on the monitor, floor by floor, alternating between utilities to show plumbing, heating, cooling, elevator shafts, electrical circuits and security aspects.

While Robyn continued to interact with Sai and the plans, moving onto the two low rise buildings. Anthony turned to Jane and Louisa and asked, "Has a site been selected for Endeavour?"

Louisa replied, "No. Not yet. We are looking for a site."

He asked, "Why draw up plans for these buildings before you have a location to build them on?"

"Firstly, to know the minimum size of the plot to acquire that would meet our requirements, and secondly to be able to visualise in sufficient detail the mechanics of precisely how all parts of Endeavour will work, and by that, I mean the academy, the enterprise centre, our headquarters, and remote backup locations. Thirdly, we also did this as a means of understanding the probability of zoning and planning permission restrictions and finally, perhaps the simplest of reasons, this was the outcome of testing what Sai can do.

Robyn exclaimed, "What we see here was a test?"

Louisa replied, "Yes. A test. At Endeavour, our core principle is that knowledge and concepts transfer, meaning that a solution to a problem, or a concept created for one purpose or area, can be transferred, repurposed, and reused for another. To do that requires a deeper understanding of the problem, the solution and the concepts. Simply put, a solution to a problem is not limited to that problem alone; it can, with further discovery, be enhanced and improved upon in order to discover deeper meaning, and further value.

"Jane and I, with Sai, designed and built tools and an application for use in marketing but we wanted to discover where those same tools and the application itself, without reinventing a new one, could be useful both to us internally and to our customers. So, we tested our theory and found further use cases, examples being, we now know how large the Endeavour maintenance team might need to be, or now as, Robyn, you have verified, a design tool for architects, engineers, surveyors, builders, and a plethora of other professions."

"This is phenomenal, and Sai is truly incredible. As an architect, I love drawing plans initially with pencil and paper, but I am an advocate for tools and technology which can make my life, and that of our clients easier. I also like to be able to manipulate a drawing and test out theories around the use of new materials, evaluate loads on a structure, assess damage control measures from tectonic shifts, natural disasters, or weather events, not to mention being able to assess and adapt changes to plans quickly for our clients, mindful of the work needed for planning permission and zoning purposes," Robyn said.

Anthony said, "When I think of all the other possible applications for this in construction and engineering and not just on the design or client facing side, even for quantity surveying purposes, pre-building planning, placement of cranes, machinery and so on. Can you even imagine the use case for this application when figuring out how to build structures on Mars? I am sorry, I know I am getting ahead of myself, but I cannot help it, the potential value is enormous."

Robyn grinned at her brother and said, "There I was thinking I was the geek about Mars. I am also getting ahead of myself."

Jane smiled and said, "I can assure you both, you have nothing whatsoever to be sorry for. Looking ahead, thinking way outside the box, and many years down the road is precisely what we do and are doing here."

Louisa said, "Jane is right. Now how about you get to really see what Sai can do?"

From there, under the guidance of Jane and Louisa with Charlie, Sam and Devon back seated around the cluster, Robyn and Anthony learned the secrets of Endeavour.

Several hours later, the Endeavour team had found a way to hide their secret, in plain sight and with the brilliant minds of an architect and engineer on board to help them do it.

****

"I think I, or indeed Sai, may have found it," Charlie exclaimed with a loud shriek of delight, gripping Michael's hand tightly where it rested on her leg, as he relaxed, seated comfortably beside her on the plush garden sofa, and talking to Sam, who was seated to his right.

Charlie's blue eyes sparkled as she looked up from her phone, at the group of men and women around her. The most brilliant of minds, the people she loved most in the world, her darling Michael, and her fellow voyagers in Endeavour.

Gathered in celebration of her birthday, they were eating grilled food from the barbeque, chatting and relaxing, enjoying late Friday evening sunshine, on the lush La Jolla garden terrace of the home which she and Michael had moved into from Pasadena, when he had retired from the bank to open his gallery, and she had officially relocated from London.

"Found what, Charlie?" Michael asked.

"I have, I believe, found the site of Endeavour," she replied.

The voices around her stopped talking, all eyes on her, their own excitement mounting.

She stood up and added, "Everyone, into the living room please, I want you all to see this."

They were all successful and driven businesspeople in their own right, so no one in the group had been surprised by how efficiently, in less than two months, they had each worked to formally establish Endeavour, a month after which they had started trading, or by how quickly Endeavour had grown over the previous nine months. Shortly into their first quarter, they had outgrown capacity at the temporary locations for the academy and the enterprise centre and were ready to scale up the business. They had each articulated their requirements for an optimal site to Sai and following the serendipitous event which had led Robyn and Anthony to Endeavour, they had moved quickly to hire Robyn and Anthony who had worked on correcting, and updating the plans, while Sai had begun to search the wider San Diego area for suitable properties.

Now with the group in pursuit behind her, Charlie hurried to the living room, switched on the large television monitor, and cast the link from her phone to it. When she was ready, she turned around to her expectant audience, taking in the wondrous sight of them all.

"Without further ado, here is a plot of unoccupied industrial property for sale, situated on multiple adjacent parcels on Kettner Boulevard, over eighty-three thousand square feet in size, former printing press site, warehouses, office space, large car park, with public transport and road access off the freeway nearby. There is a virtual tour, and then we can look at the maps."

Charlie slowly scrolled through the description, then played the virtual tour, which consisted of aerial footage, and a detailed look at each of the parcels of land. The buildings appeared to be in a state of neglect and disrepair, remnants of the previous occupier still visible, boxes covered in dust, a forgotten office chair and desks here and there.

When the virtual tour ended, Andrea said, "Charlie, in my capacity as advisor on matters of strategy, I know that we have rapidly outgrown our temporary premises, and why we need to find a permanent home for Endeavour, and our clients, but my advice on that property is to buy it, knock it down and then rebuild it."

Everyone nodded and laughed at the easy, straightforward way in which Andrea had stated what they had all thought. Peggy, her operations mind analysing what she had seen on the virtual tour, was thinking about access to the enterprise centre, where the outdoor trade shows and market stalls could go, and how accessible the site was to the academy, to the nearest bus, and light rail station. She said, "I can see why this property is of interest, Charlie. Can we take a look at the site map and plans, please?"

Charlie opened the site map and plans side by side on the large screen. There was silence in the room as each of them absorbed what they were seeing in the context of their own business interest and area within Endeavour.

Jane pulled out her phone, sent the link to a secure location for Sai to analyse and harvest information from, quickly issued instructions to Sai on her phone and turned her attention back to the television monitor to evaluate the site for geological constraints, site elevation for telecommunications and power sources, logistics, distance and connectivity from the underground data centres to the adjacent sites and the remote backup locations.

Devon was assessing zoning and building restrictions from what he saw on screen about the property. If the site was found to be the right one, he had all the information he needed with which to file the paperwork.

David was considering the proximity of it to their temporary site. He also wondered what happened to all of the people who had worked for the printing press, when a thought occurred to him, so he took out his phone, and assisted by Sai, did some research.

Amy was assessing implications of a move to a new location on Endeavour's coaching staff, the students and the enterprise centre clients and staff there. As she looked around the room at the beautiful minds of the people around her, she considered the stress and extra work that each of them would need to handle and deal with over the next few months and year or so ahead. She, with her exquisite mind, was already building a plan for how to help and coach them, and mapping out the set of tasks and sequences of the tasks that would put the plan into motion.

Louisa evaluated different tiers of inward and outward communications that would be needed across all parts of Endeavour. She smiled to herself at the prospect of the work ahead.

Charlie was deep in thought about the opportunities she saw with the site, the economic viability of it, and how long they would be waiting for the permissions needed to clear and rebuild on the site.

Sam was visualising and calculating what Endeavour's balance sheets would look like over the next ten and twenty years, and what adjustments to them would look like following acquisition and redevelopment of this site for their purposes.

Michael, breaking the silence, said, "Though the price tag seems low to me, it is still a significant outlay cost. However, given how profitable Endeavour already is, it seems to me that this site, at face value, even with estimated filing, legal, financing and construction costs could pay for itself in less than ten years. I expect there will be room for negotiation on the price. If I were not so comfortable lounging here with all of you, I would be tempted to go to see it now."

Everyone laughed at the last part of his sentence, particularly as they were just as comfortable as he but equally keen to visit the site.

Sam said, "It is an ideal site for Endeavour. It fits the criteria of what we have been looking for very well and is within range of what we expected. Considering the location of the site, it seems undervalued to me too, but I say we gather as much intel as we can and move to act on this site as quickly as possible."

"Agreed. I will put in a call to the real estate company now, if they answer, find out who the seller is and arrange a site visit," Devon said.

"Devon, we won't need to do that. The seller, and owner is Mr Jonathan Willis, who we all know as Jon Willis. I have messaged him. When do we want to go to see the site?" David asked.

Charlie said, "How… Of course, the printing press… I knew Jon owned property, but I did not know that site was one of them. This is simply wonderful, David, and due credit to you for the quick thinking in making the connection to Jon. I have messaged both Robyn and Anthony. Jane, I have told them to wait for an update from Sai."

In response to the brief and wonderful pause from everyone, Amy said, "Not only have we found a possible location for Endeavour, but we have once again seen the spirit of Endeavour. David, I did not know I needed a reminder of what independent action can do, or how each action, each step, powers forward motion toward what it is we are setting out to achieve, and how magnificent it is to see, and how good it is to feel the benefits of that motion. Thank you, David, for a reminder that I did not know I needed."

"Why thank you, Amy, and I suppose I needed to hear that reminder played back to me too," David said.

Charlie said, "It's so true, Amy. We all embody that spirit, I am proud every time I see and hear it, and I thank you for calling it out. David, to answer your question, can we arrange a site visit for tomorrow morning, the earlier the better? It is a holiday weekend; the academy will be closed, and the enterprise centre is equipped to function without us. I imagine this will be an entire group trip?"

To a loud chorus of yesses, which included Michael, Charlie smiled and said, "Jane, given that we may have the location, can you have Sai render up revised blueprints for this site overlaid with what you, Robyn and Louisa already drew up for us, and send them to Robyn and Anthony, please? Louisa, Amy, Devon, we will need to enact the plan we created to mitigate against potential planning objections so can you work together to examine local population demographics, schools, other local employers and businesses as we agreed?"

"Of course, Charlie, I am already on it. Data is incoming and will be shared," Louisa said.

Jane said, "Sai is already working on the revised plans. They will be with Robyn and Anthony shortly. Now I don't know about anyone else, but I am still hungry and before our school outing tomorrow, I think a celebration is in order."

Amy said, "On that note of celebration, Michael, for the other endeavour, now seems like a very good time."

"Indeed, it is," he replied with a grin.

Michael moved toward the beautifully radiant Charlie where she stood in front of them, and with pride and love for himself and her, he proposed to her, which she, without pause or question, accepted. In love and joy at her reply, surrounded by the love of their closest friends, they celebrated the promise they had made to each other in London, all those years ago.

Sam said, "Michael and Charlie, the truest superheroes of change that I have ever known, to the greatest architects of love, and of Endeavour, we love and celebrate you both." Then he grinned broadly and added, "And yes, Michael, I will be your best man, David and Devon your groomsmen and in case you think we were unprepared, just know we already have orders in for our top-hats and tailcoats."

David chimed in and said with a grin, "We do, we placed the orders months ago but, Sam, we agreed, you weren't actually supposed to tell Michael that."

Michael replied with a smile, "Well, Charlie, it seems that we will not require any wedding planners as these fine gentlemen have it in hand. What say you that we leave them to it?"

Charlie laughed and said, "That is a splendid idea, Michael. To whichever of you is the chief planner, here is some simple guidance from me: I am marrying Michael; my doing so requires no embellishment, only celebration of all that brought us together, what we have already accomplished together and what we will continue to do together over the years ahead."

Michael turned to her and said, "My beautiful bride to be, I love you."

CHAPTER ELEVEN - SIGHT OF LOVE

Michael Weston and his beautiful wife, Charlie Rochford Weston, were nestled up close together, sitting up whilst sipping coffee under the covers of the bed of the very same room, of the very same hotel in London where they had met for the first time, many years ago. They had married many months before with a beautiful civil ceremony followed by a lavish party, surrounded by family and friends, but had waited until the final Endeavour building had been completed to go on honeymoon, their chosen destination for which was Monte Carlo and the south coast of France, followed by a weekend stopover in London before flying home to the United States.

He loved to watch and sketch her as she watched the sunrise. The way the light was cast on her face, the way she tilted her head towards it as if she could feel the warmth of it, taking strength from it, was to his eyes, a vision of a goddess.

"Charlie, you are a goddess."

She turned her face toward him, smiled, looked at the sketch he had drawn of her and said, "It is true, I am. Though, I love you, Michael, not for falling at my feet in adoration and worship of my goddess status but for standing proudly by my side where I can see, hear, feel and touch you, and you can see and touch me. Also, can you just imagine how skewed the perspective of that sketch would be, if all you could ever do was look up at me, or only from a distance?"

He said huskily, "I enjoy watching you from a distance as when I do, it inspires me, and as for looking up at you, my darling, well I relish and wilfully savour that too."

She smiled at him, took his coffee cup from his hand, and set it down with hers on the bedside table, kissing him as she slowly moved her naked body onto his and said impishly, "Like this you mean? Is this the only sight that you want to savour?"

Pulling her closer to him, he replied, "Yes and no. I relish every inch of your beautiful body, my darling, but the inches I savour cannot be seen, only felt."

Feeling the thrust of him, she moaned in euphoric pleasure and whispered in his ear, "I savour it too."

They basked, as lovers do, in the close, tender aftermath, in the glow of their shared pleasure, and reminisced on all they had seen, done and achieved together. They talked about what awaited them both back at home, the pride, the anticipation and excitement, the love of moving forward and doing more, to achieve even more.

Later, as they had packed their bags and prepared to leave for the airport, when they reached the elevator where they had met for the very first time, seeing the sculpture still standing on the table, Charlie turned to Michael and said, "Michael, you are the boldest and proudest endeavour of my life."

"You were a sight to my eyes when I first met you right here, and you are the truest product of meaningful endeavour to me too."

CHAPTER TWELVE - BLIND SIGHT

Sara Goodwin was working in the office space just behind reception, when the security camera feed showed a car, with a male driver and a female passenger, pulling into the reserved by appointment only slot in front of Endeavour headquarters. As they got out of the car, she noticed the woman was talking on her phone and did not appear at all happy. She could not pinpoint what it was exactly about the pair that stood out to her as she watched them begin to walk from the car toward the front door of Endeavour but she sensed trouble.

Keeping an eye on the camera feed, and the front door, she checked the visitor schedule for Endeavour, for Charlie and the team, for Robyn and Anthony's office on the top floor but there were no appointments scheduled for at least the next hour. *This is very odd*, she thought to herself, because following the continued reports over the course of several weeks, of unusual spikes in online chatter about Endeavour, they had acted swiftly and had taken precautionary measures across the entire business. Using Sai to trace and monitor the activity, they had pinpointed the epicentre of the activity to a location in Sacramento and they had observed a rippling effect, which had spread across the country. Endeavour had responded by tightening their cyber and building security monitoring. Even before they had taken such precautions, last minute same day appointments and not using the visitor booking system were both unheard of at Endeavour.

Sara glanced at the camera feed and briefly considered reserving her judgement until the two visitors had reached and had spoken to her, but she calculated she had less than two minutes before that happened, so she decided to act and decisively so.

She issued multiple instructions to Sai and sent a brief message to Charlie and the management team which said, 'Two people just arrived at HQ, no visitors due. Erring on the side of caution, Sai is now on alert observation mode. I will redirect to the academy, if needed, and once further information is available.'

Jane, who had seen the change to Sai's mode, replied instantly, 'Thank you Sara, I see them.'

Sam replied, 'A prudent move Sara, thank you for buying us time.'

As the two visitors approached Sara at reception, the woman was just ending her call, and Sara caught the words, "Calm down, Edward. I need to go. Terry and I will update you tomorrow."

Sara, with a courteous smile and professional tone of voice, said, "Welcome to Endeavour, may I take your names and who you are here to see?"

The man spoke and gruffly introduced himself as Mr Terrence Wickes from a state education committee, the name for which Sara could not decipher. The woman introduced herself as Ms Kathleen Green, the dean of the Marshall Social Institute of Education, a semi-private university upstate and added, "We do not have an appointment, we are here to see the board of directors of this company on a matter of great importance."

"I see. Ms Green, Mr Wickes, the board of directors of Endeavour are all working over at the academy today. If you would like to leave your contact details with me, I am happy to arrange an appointment for you to meet with them on a more suitable day."

"No, that is not acceptable to us. We must meet with them today," Mr Wickes said.

Pausing for a moment with intended deliberation, Sara handed them a digital tablet each and said, "As you wish, Mr Wickes. However, I will need to issue you with visitor badges. We operate to a very strict security policy here at Endeavour so if I could ask you both to fill out the simple form on those tablets, the information you provide will be used to process your security profile and badges, and that will take less than a minute. While I do that, Ms Green, Mr Wickes, to find the academy, as you exit this building, turn to your right and follow the way-marked footpath which will lead you right to it. I will notify the directors to expect you both."

They completed the forms, handed the tablets back, and Sara, true to her word, processed their profiles, printed and gave them their visitors' badges and wished them a pleasant day, by which point Sai and the Endeavour team had the minimum amount of information needed to find out more about their visitors.

Ms Green and Mr Wickes had only just turned away from reception when Sara was tagged in a message from Charlie to the group saying, 'From all of us, thank you Sara for trusting your instinct and acting as you did. You handled that like the true professional that you are. John and Devon are both beaming like proud fathers who have trained you well.' Sara responded with, 'Thank you Charlie. Sai has already collated further information, which is stored and ready for retrieval to be acted upon.'

In the time that it had taken Ms Green and Mr Wickes to reach the academy, the Endeavour team had gathered, and were equipped with information about these unexpected visitors who had demanded their time, as if it was theirs by right to demand.

Devon was waiting for them as they stepped inside the building and went to greet them with a professional demeanour and with his courtroom tone said, "Ms Green, Mr Wickes, I am Devon Forsyth, chief of legal affairs here at Endeavour. I understand from Sara that though you did not have an appointment, you have a matter of importance to discuss with the board which required us to interrupt our work?"

"That is correct, Mr Forsyth," Ms Green answered.

"I see. May I ask for a brief summary of what the matter of importance is?"

Mr Wickes replied, "It is something which we think will be of great interest to Endeavour."

"I see. Do you have a written brief with you, which the board and I can review as you talk?"

Mr Wickes answered, "No. We did not think that would be necessary at this stage."

"I see. Mr Wickes, you referred to a 'we' in both of your responses, may I ask who exactly the 'we' is?"

Ms Green said, "Mr Wickes represents the state education committee, and I am the dean of the Marshall Social Institute of Education, a semi-private university upstate. Perhaps you have heard of us, Mr Forsyth?"

"I cannot say that I have, Ms Green."

Devon paused and said, "Mr Wickes, Ms Green, if you

would both like to follow me, I will show you to the conference room. As a matter of due diligence, I will require you both to sign an indemnity non-disclosure agreement, which will prohibit the use of and disclosure of, by you, or the bodies you represent, any information about Endeavour or its activities which is not already in the public domain. Further to which, I have a waiver which states that the board's agreement to meet with you is at your unscheduled request and does not imply or constitute any form of agreement by Endeavour, to the terms of what it is you wish to discuss or how you, or the bodies you represent, operate. Are you authorised to sign these two documents?"

"Mr Forsyth, of course we are authorised to sign them," Mr Wickes smugly replied.

"Very well."

As Devon guided the visitors upstairs, he politely explained how the academy building used to be a printing press warehouse, and that the enterprise and trade centre stood where the printing factory used to be, while the headquarters building which they had just come from, was built from new. He described how both of the older buildings were empty, and wasted with neglect, when they had purchased them but had been rebuilt from the ground up and the site was, he said with pride, far from empty and neglected now.

"It has been a miracle for the local community, Mr Forsyth," Mr Wickes said.

"That is an interesting turn of phrase, what do you mean by a miracle, Mr Wickes?"

Mr Wickes answered, "There are more people from this immediate community returning to work than anywhere else in the county. Teachers in our schools have reported that literacy, numeracy rates and other basic skills amongst children, young adults and their parents have improved. Students from this academy who dropped out of their university courses without any qualification are beating graduates with degrees and qualifications in the job market. It is putting our students at an unfair disadvantage and making our schools look bad."

Devon looked at Mr Wickes curiously, as they arrived at the conference room, where he opened the door for them and said, "Is that so, Mr Wickes? We were not aware of any such miracle but that was very useful information. Please take a seat anywhere you like, and I will be right back with the paperwork which you agreed to sign and then with my fellow directors."

Devon stepped into a nearby office where Charlie, Michael, the rest of the team and John Cooper were gathered because it had a printer, and a monitor connected to the internal security application, which Jane, John, Devon and Sara had been working on with Sai. The application leveraged new custom-built, real-time audio, camera feed and facial recognition processing tools which had provided the team with a means of monitoring the entire conversation, from the moment Devon had greeted the visitor's downstairs, to when he had shown them into the conference room. Not only were they pleased with the output, they were pleased to have performed a first and very real test, which had delivered invaluable information and placed that at their disposal in real time.

Sam asked, "Now that we have a reasonable idea of who these people are, though the specifics of why they are here are not clear, could this event be the basis for the case we discussed earlier, Andrea, Devon?"

Andrea nodded and Devon replied, "As soon as they, and Charlie you, sign those agreements, then we may have grounds. This is an unwarranted visit, but we cannot fall foul of jumping to conclusions, when we do require specific information on why they are here."

Sam asked, "Could we be accused of attempting to censor information?"

Devon replied, "This visit to us is not a coincidence. It is premeditated, by virtue of the fact they are here but we were not given any notice of their intention. They clearly want something which we have and were sent here to get it, under the illusion that because they want it, by whatever authority they think they have, or represent, that we will give it. If either were to think about why our first action was to have them sign an agreement prohibiting any disclosure of information and how we took that measure so quickly, then an attempt to construe it as censorship could be made.

"However, we are a privately owned company; outside of filing tax return information, how we operate, and what the precise nature of Endeavour is, in law, our intellectual property. We are under no legal obligation, beyond those already stated, to disclose our intellectual property, or information about ourselves, or our business without our consent, noting that we grant that consent to customers, and they to us, when we enter into mutually defined business agreements with them. We have no such agreement here."

Charlie was deep in thought, visualising pathways in her mind and said, "That we do not, Devon. Though you are right about not falling foul of jumping to conclusions, I am going to leap to one anyway and say that we will need John with us. Can we introduce him as an advisor to the board?"

"Yes," he replied.

To John, Charlie said, "John, we are all well equipped for the task at hand but you excel at independently getting to details and assembling evidence in a way that may well, I find, be necessary in this situation, and though I hope we will never need to act upon it, it is better to be prepared. Do I have your agreement to act as an advisor to the board for this purpose?"

"Yes, Charlie. You have my full and absolute agreement. You all do."

"Thank you, John," Charlie said.

Amy picked up the documents to be signed from the printer, handed them to her husband and said, "I know we are not used to printed documents any more, and that this is, by Endeavour standards, unusual, but there are behavioural markers associated with being passed physical objects, in this case documents, which Devon you from your courtroom days, will be able to observe, and of course we do want to give them every opportunity to read them, ask questions and then choose not to sign them."

Devon quickly nodded at his wife, left the room, and went back down the corridor into the conference room. Passing the visitors the two documents, he said, "Mr Wickes, Ms Green, before I introduce you to the board who will be here momentarily, here is the indemnity non-disclosure agreement and the waiver that we discussed. Please review them carefully, and if you have any questions, I will be right here if you need to consult me, and there is no fee at this time for provisioning you with my services."

Mr Wickes and Ms Green reviewed the documents in turn, neither asked any questions nor made any comments and then using the pen provided by Devon, they both signed the two documents. He advised that once Ms Rochford had signed them too, copies would be made for both of them, and if they granted permission, he would email the signed documents to them for electronic record keeping purposes, to which both granted their consent, and Devon thanked them for their cooperation.

Just as he did so, Charlie and the rest of the team walked into the conference room and sat down. Devon introduced the visitors to Charlie by saying, "Ms Green, Mr Wickes, may I present Ms Charlotte Rochford, chief executive of Endeavour. Ms Rochford will introduce you to everyone here."

Charlie began by formally introducing the team while she signed the documents that Devon had slid towards her. She concluded her introduction by saying, "Mr Wickes, Ms Green, it is unfortunate that we were indisposed when you arrived, however, we had no record of an appointment made to see us today. As we are eleven of the coaches here at the academy, your unscheduled visit required us to make arrangements."

With a shocked expression, Mr Wickes asked, "Are you saying, Ms Rochford, that you, and everyone sitting here with us now, works in the academy?"

"Yes."

"But who runs and manages the business when you are teaching?"

"We do."

"But you are the board of directors?"

"Yes."

"Why are you not paying people who need jobs to do the work for you?"

"We do not pay people to do our own work for us."

"You are not employing people who are qualified to teach?"

"What qualifications do you mean and to teach what?"

"Teachers who are qualified to follow a pre-approved curriculum."

"We do not require a curriculum, pre-approved or otherwise, nor teachers who only know how to follow one."

"What could you possibly expect to teach people without a curriculum?"

"That a person who acts on their own initiative, on their own authority, at their own pace, to learn and who works for their own purpose and enjoyment, not causing harm to another, is to be welcomed, encouraged, and is not to be punished or curtailed in any way for doing so."

"But what about the standards, the rules, the policies, processes and procedures that you need in order to run a company and manage people?"

"There are externally prescribed rules and regulations over which we have no control; we adhere to them, but they do not inform how we operate Endeavour. The success of Endeavour has not been achieved using force or duress. We are looking for individuals, and not, Mr Wickes, a collection of robots or machines whose only purpose is to follow instruction. We have technology for the latter, which cannot and will not truly replace or remove the need for the former. Guidance serves a fundamental purpose to our business; we use technology to achieve that guidance. Rules, internally prescribed rules, standards, policies, or procedures, when or if there is no context or understanding of what they are designed to do, serve no purpose or value to Endeavour, the people who work here, or our customers. People who work with us already have their own standards, and we respect them. If a person who comes to work with Endeavour finds a way, for instance, even by error, of completing a task in two hours which had otherwise taken two days, and that was achieved by them identifying a workaround or a different or improved solution, through examination, researching the problem or task, understanding the causes and effects, asking questions and seeking help where needed, that person will be rewarded not punished. Do we insist or demand that this person sit at a desk for seven, or eight hours every day? No. Do we encourage this person to learn, discover, explore more about themselves, and Endeavour, and bring their wonderful minds, their skills and experience, what they know, to as many parts of Endeavour as they are interested in, or if they choose to go elsewhere? Yes."

"How can you possibly think you can run a business in this way, and want to be successful?"

"Endeavour is successful."

"Who says so?"

"I do."

"I do not understand."

"I am aware of that."

Charlie asked, "Ms Green, Mr Wickes, I understand from your conversation with Sara that you have a matter of importance to discuss with us. May I ask you to explain to us what that matter is?"

Ms Green spoke and said, "Ms Rochford, it has come to the attention of the state committee of education which Mr Wickes represents and to the board of the university which I am dean of, that this company has become a public institution and a godsend to the local community."

"What do you mean?" Charlie asked.

"As I explained to Mr Forsyth on the way up here, it has been a miracle for the local community, Ms Rochford," Mr Wickes said.

"How so, Mr Wickes?"

Mr Wickes answered by repeating word for word what he had said to Devon earlier on their way up to the conference room.

"Mr Wickes, Ms Green, is that the matter of importance which you declared you wanted to discuss with us?" Charlie asked.

"Not directly," Ms Green replied.

"Can you, Ms Green, in that case, please tell us what the matter of importance is?"

Ms Green replied, "Well, Ms Rochford. The board of the university has unanimously agreed that it would like to acquire an equity stake in this company in exchange for a partnership with the university. In addition, the state committee of education which Mr Wickes represents would like to offer the company a package of incentives to reward the business for the work it is actively doing in the community."

So this is the day, Charlie thought, as she looked at Michael, who she saw was watching her, reading her expression, a smile on his face as they both recalled the words he had said to her about this day, that they would laugh, firstly because they both knew then it would happen, and secondly, in the time it would take for them to realise that you are a threat, he had said, you and Endeavour will already have succeeded. She and Michael had replayed that conversation with the team many times, and they, with much guidance from Amy, had prepared as best they could for the high probability of such a scenario, just like the one facing them now, occurring.

Moving her eyes away from Michael, she looked around the table at John and then at her fellow founders. She was proud to see ten composed, proudly defiant but inquisitive faces looking from her to the two visitors. She smiled when she saw Sam wink at her. *Let's do this*, she thought.

Charlie turned her attention to the visitors, and she said, "Endeavour is not for sale. We do not require partners or investors. We will not entertain any discussion whatsoever on incentives. If there is nothing further, Ms Green, Mr Wickes, I have—"

Mr Wickes interrupted, "You cannot possibly say that Ms Rochford? You have not heard any details."

"I have said it, and you are right about details, Mr Wickes, I did not hear any," Charlie replied plainly.

"If you could hear us out, Ms Rochford. I am sure you will see this is a great opportunity," Mr Wickes said.

"An opportunity, Mr Wickes, is defined as a time or set of circumstances that makes it possible to do something. There is no opportunity here."

"But you are, by our records, a recently established business, approximately seven years old, which provides a public service. The government likes to get involved in supporting business, it is good for the public, and for the community as a whole. It is ludicrous that you are outrightly rejecting an offer which would be good for the community and would serve the public interest. Why are you doing this? I cannot understand it." Mr Wickes asked, glancing at Ms Green to his right and then with puzzlement at Charlie.

She replied evenly, "I am certain that the board here will have questions on the particulars of your statement; however, I do not, but I will restate the position of this company once again." She continued, "Endeavour is, and will remain, a wholly owned private company. I have no concern if you opt to describe this company as a public service; the term has no meaning to me considering that companies are usually in business to sell products or services to a customer base which is usually made up of the public. We will neither apply for, nor be induced into applying, or accepting any form of external incentive to keep Endeavour in operation because we do not need any.

Charlie paused for a moment, and proceeded to say, "Endeavour, or any part of it, is not for sale. We are in business to serve our own interests, which is to make a profit, and in a way that we will remain profitable over the next five, ten, and twenty years. We do that by selling services in exchange for a price that is commensurate with our costs, our margin, and the value which by paying us, our customers will receive. In doing so, we work with our customers to help them understand how what we have sold them increases their value, which provides them with the opportunity, by their own choice, to sell their services commensurate with their costs and updated value back to us, and to do so for a price which serves their own interests and reasons. We do not give, or receive, any kind of service for free, because to do so undermines our own value, and that of our customers. We do not need to be told what our value is, we know what our value is, we understand every precise component of it, and the price attached to each part."

"But this is preposterous, you are making a judgement without hearing any detail, and it is unheard of for the chief executive of a modern company, to not mention anything whatsoever about your obligations towards the community, and wanting to do more for the community, by accepting a proposal which would ease the burden of you doing that," Ms Green said.

Devon, interjected, "Madam, it is legally and financially sound to make a judgement on a case when there is no evidence presented to support it. Furthermore, outside of taxes, there is no legal obligation on Endeavour to do so, toward a burden it does not have nor will have in the future. Lastly, Ms Rochford is not the chief executive of what you may class as a modern company. She is so much more than that, proudly and rightly so – she is the chief executive of Endeavour."

Charlie smiled, nodded her approval and gratitude toward Devon, her gesture mirrored by the team, as he concluded the last part.

Sam said, "Ms Green, Mr Wickes, Ms Rochford has clearly and rightly stated the position of Endeavour. However, I am not clear on the details of what exactly you are both doing here, or why it is that you think that your suggestion would be of interest to this board. Would you mind if John, the team, and I asked you some questions about your proposal to help us understand the details of it?"

"Yes, by all means, Mr Walker," Ms Green replied abrasively.

"Thank you, Ms Green. Firstly, are you aware that Endeavour is a wholly owned, private company, which means the shares are held largely by the owners in this room and that as Endeavour has not made a public debt offering, we are not under any legal obligation to publish information, other than articles of incorporation for the state that we are incorporated in, or publish financial reports with any federal or state agency, other than for tax filing purposes?

"No, Mr Walker. I was not aware of that," Ms Green replied.

"Nor I, Mr Walker," Mr Wickes said.

Sam said, "I see. Then how familiar are you, and Mr Wickes, with what it is that we do here at Endeavour?

Ms Green replied, "I am not familiar with the details of the company, Mr Walker, however, I understand Endeavour is a trade school of some description."

Michael asked calmly, "Ms Green, I would like to clarify a point with you please. You and Mr Wickes came here today to meet the board, and specifically to tell us about a wish to acquire a stake in the company but you are not familiar with the company which is the focus of that acquisition?

"That is correct, Mr Weston. The details of the company do not matter. The university, and our stakeholders, and the state are more interested in taking an active, guiding, partnering role in the work that you do for the community here, and expand it elsewhere," she replied.

Sam looked at Michael, then Charlie, then at Peggy and continued around the table to see serious faces amongst the entire Endeavour team. He thought back to the day when he and Peggy, thanks to the call he had received from Michael, had finally met Charlie and then Jane and David for the first time. He recalled the following day, at his home, when he and Peggy had hosted the full group, for their first meeting, where every discussion, about their own lives, their own businesses and that of Endeavour was founded on detail, evidence, reason, and fact.

Such was the almost luxurious atmosphere which they had created within their group, and enjoyed within Endeavour, as a place to work, to trade, to thrive, to live and love every day, that he had almost forgotten that there was a whole other world out there, where workplaces were not pleasant places to be, that somehow details, reason and proactive decision making were deemed irrelevant to running a business. He had forgotten how many times he had seen business cases, plans, and reports, with lots of words but which said nothing of any value, and were entirely devoid of detail, evidence, or facts, and always reminded him of the story of the emperor's new clothes.

He braced himself as he said, "Ms Green, you stated a wish by the university to acquire an equity stake in Endeavour, which leads me to ask the following: by what method was a valuation of Endeavour derived? What was the resulting valuation in monetary terms? And what percentage of equity stake? You also stated that the equity stake would be in exchange for a partnership of some kind; how was the value of a partnership with the university derived?"

Ms Green replied, "Why speak in such crude monetary terms, Mr Walker? If you only care to speak in them however, we are seeking twenty percent of Endeavour. Furthermore, money is no object to the university or to the state, both are well funded."

As Sam absorbed her answer, he silently thanked himself for his previous train of thought about the world outside of Endeavour, then he said calmly, "Ms Green, Endeavour is a business; monetary and value terms are the terms by which we operate this company. You say, Ms Green, that the university is well funded but from published financial records, it is running at a loss and has been for many years, as is the parent group which your university belongs to.

"You say that the state is well funded, but it is also running at a loss, and it is no secret that it has been for many years. If the university moved towards acquiring even a five-percent stake in Endeavour, doing so would bankrupt the university and the parent company; acquiring twenty percent of Endeavour is not conceivable, Ms Green. Even if you were to somehow raise capital via investors or borrow from the state to fund the acquisition, neither the taxpayers in this state nor the investors would ever see a return, and part of our business would also be gone, which would do irrevocable damage. Ms Green, if you want to save and protect the university, all your students and employees, and Mr Wickes, if you want to protect the state from further debt, I recommend you review your position that either are well-funded."

Ms Green asked, "How could you possibly know that for certain, Mr Walker?"

Sam said, "Because, Ms Green, I have been working in financial treasury for over thirty years, the basic rule for which is that, when it comes to the management of money, debt and finances, be it for an individual, a household, a company, a state or an entire country, details do in fact matter.

"The evaluation of balance sheets and financial information over a period of time cannot hide the fact, or the risk, that if expenditure is more than income, and there are no reserves or savings to cover the difference, and that same cycle is repeated year after year, the result will be financial ruin and collapse, with often far reaching consequences. Endeavour Academy here has proudly welcomed over five-hundred-thousand customers through its doors, just under seventy percent of whom have subscribed to the financial planning and management courses, which I and my team deliver, because those customers were either on the receiving end of those consequences, or were facing financial ruin themselves. The hardest lesson for them to learn is to stop ignoring facts, details and the precise reality of their situation."

"That seems like a very unfortunate situation for those people, but I still do not see why this company is helping people who are failing in their lives, or why these people come here instead of seeking help from the state or becoming qualified by going to a proper school," Mr Wickes said.

Ms Green nodded and said, "Mr Walker, I agree with Mr Wickes, and the situation for these very irresponsible people is very different to that of the university because the university cannot fail."

Sam replied, "Evidence exists which contradicts both of your statements, Mr Wickes, Ms Green. Neither I, nor this board, nor our customers can ignore the evidence, as to do so would mark the end of Endeavour and dare I say it, the end of me too."

Charlie was tracking the conversation carefully, updating pathways in her mind as she processed new information and new insights. In doing so, she spotted an opportunity, which she knew would put her, and Endeavour, on another collision course with the state, but which over the longer term could expand Endeavour, and could even, she thought, limit the far reaching consequences of what was going to happen if Ms Green, and the board of the university, continued to believe that they could not fail, though the evidence indicated that the failure was already past, and not future tense. She used her phone to send a brief message to Sam and the group, quickly outlined the opportunity, to which she observed subtle nods of approval in response. As there was little else to be achieved from the meeting, other than having John understand the circumstances which led to their visit, Charlie just really wanted to wrap it up, and so she said, "Ms Green, Mr Wickes, there is information, which is freely available in the public domain, on what it is that Endeavour does. Would it be of help to you if I provided you with a summary of it?"

"Yes, Ms Rochford. I suppose that could be of help," Mr Wickes replied.

Charlie described the types and prices of day or evening courses which customers to the academy could avail of, using cooking, computer skills, website and graphic design, financial planning, budgeting, tax returns, business planning and administration, as examples. She explained they had a wide range of individuals from various backgrounds and occupations, who were either customers of the academy, or were working with Endeavour as coaches, from former police officers, bank managers, military veterans, doctors, scientists, early school leavers, university graduates, stay at home parents, truck drivers, nurses to engineers. She also described the function of the Endeavour Enterprise and Trade Centre and summarised the types of traders and other services which Endeavour provided to those businesses.

"That is quite a mix of a business, Ms Rochford, and you say these people are either coaches, students or traders?" Ms Green asked.

"Yes," Charlie replied.

David added, "Often, Ms Green, they are all three."

"How long has the academy been open now?" Mr Wickes asked.

"At this site, five years."

"The enterprise centre?"

"The same."

"Where did all these people come from?" Mr Wickes asked.

David answered, "There are many answers to that question, Mr Wickes. The easiest way to answer it, however, is to ask at least one of them. Mr Cooper here for instance, a former police lieutenant, who took early retirement, what was it John, seven or eight years ago now?"

"Correct, eight years ago."

"You were in the police force?" Ms Green asked.

"Yes, ma'am. For thirty-five years."

"Why did you take early retirement?"

"I loved my work, ma'am, but I was tired of fighting battles which, I eventually realised, I could not win."

"What kinds of battles?" Mr Wickes asked.

"I would rather not discuss that, sir."

"What did you do after you left the police force?"

"I spent the first three months enjoying my retirement, golfing, fishing, sailing, getting all the jobs done around the house that had needed to be done for years, and enjoying time with my wife Annie, our children and grandchildren. Soon, however, I realised that though I was happy with my decision to retire from the police force, there was something missing. It was Annie who suggested that I try to find a new job. She was right. I missed earning my own keep and being truly productive at something I enjoy. At the time, I thought that I could maybe do something in security, or private investigations, or even a legal department, something like that, so I contacted many recruitment agents, even those that I had dealt with over the years in policing, to go about finding a job. David's recruitment firm was the only one to respond."

"At your age, Mr Cooper, that was brave," Mr Wickes said.

"That is not a surprising viewpoint, Mr Wickes. Utilising Mr Banner's services, I started to reshape my resume, and turn the experience acquired during my career in the police force into skills that could prove beneficial to an employer. I lost count of how many jobs I had applied for. Many applications seemed to go into a void and neither David nor I had any success in determining where they had gone, or what had happened to them. For many others, I got to the interview stage, but was unsuccessful. The reasons given were many: they felt I was too old, overqualified, underqualified, that I was not the right fit with the culture of the company; they felt I would not be able to take instruction or direction.

"As a police officer, I spent much of my career interviewing suspects in criminal investigations, the first rule of which is that feelings are not admissible as evidence or permitted in a court of law. A feeling is not proof, evidence or a reason. On attempting to make enquiries about the actual reasons, they often told me they were not at liberty to say, as it was not company policy. It was a tough experience at the time but in hindsight, it was a valuable one."

"How long have you been here?"

"From the very first day Endeavour opened its doors at its previous site."

"How did you find out about it?"

"David called me a month or so before it opened. He told me about the plans for the academy as a place for people to further themselves and explore new skills. I had nothing to lose and everything to gain so I agreed. I have had many wonderful memorable days in my life, the evening I met Annie for the first time at a jazz club downtown, then our wedding day, every day I have spent with her since, and then there was the day when David, introduced me to Ms Rochford, and the brilliant group of people sitting here at this table."

"I do not see what is so special about Endeavour," Mr Wickes said.

"There is nothing special about Endeavour until you choose to consider what you are comparing it with, and the criteria you are using to do so," John replied.

"What do you do here, Mr Cooper?" Ms Green asked.

"For the most part I am a coach, and for my role, I work with Ms Adams, over there in the technology department and often with Mr Forsyth in the legal department."

"You work with the technology team? What makes you qualified to work in technology?" Ms Green asked.

John replied, "I do not have a computer science degree if that is what you mean. Before I started here, my understanding of technology was, or so I thought, limited to being able to operate a computer, my phone and the applications I needed in my job. It was

Ms Rochford, Ms Adams, and Mrs Forsyth who, with some simple questions, guided me to recognise that I, with my knowledge and experience, would be of far more value to advancing technology, than I could ever have possibly imagined. Granted, there was much I did not know, so I spent months with Ms Adams learning as much as I could, and she learned from me. I have not looked back since, because I am working with a company that I love, in a role that I absolutely love, and doing things in a way that I love. My wife Annie is a retired nurse, who now also works with Endeavour and teaches cookery classes to people and families of all ages, which she absolutely loves."

With a distinct tone of animosity, Mr Wickes said, "I can't think how a retired police officer could be of any use to technology."

"Someday, Mr Wickes, you will think back to this very meeting and remember making that statement to me and desperately wish you hadn't."

"I didn't mean to offend you, Mr Cooper," Mr Wickes commented.

"You did not offend me, Mr Wickes, because I have reason to know, without question, that the statement is not true. There are many people of all ages, backgrounds, and occupations here at Endeavour, who also have solid reason to know that the statement you made does not apply to them. Your statement, Mr Wickes, was not a reflection on me," John said.

John looked at his phone briefly and said, "Ms Green, Mr Wickes, if you do not have any further questions for me, I would like to ask you about the circumstances which brought you both to Endeavour today. Ms Rochford, and Mr Walker have stated the position of Endeavour in respect to the equity stake acquisition and incentive package which you have alluded to during your visit so far. Given your own statements that neither of you were familiar with Endeavour when you arrived, which we have worked to correct, it is reasonable that the board have the opportunity to be furnished with sufficient reciprocal information, and as a reminder, the information disclosed here is bound by the same indemnity non-disclosure agreement."

Ms Green signalled him to go ahead, and Mr Wickes said, "Ask what you like, Mr Cooper."

John asked, "Ms Green, could you provide some background information on the Marshall Social Institute of Education? For example, how many students are enrolled there, for what fields of study, and how many are on faculty staff?"

She replied easily, "The Marshall Social Institute of Education in Sacramento, California was opened in nineteen-ninety-five, and is equipped for seven hundred students. Faculties are grouped into social sciences and teaching, the most popular areas of study are political science, economics, and education. We currently have four-hundred students enrolled and maintain a full staff of one-hundred and fifty people."

"You have come a very long way from Sacramento, Ms Green. How did you come to hear about Endeavour that led you to travel down here?" John asked.

Ms Green said, "About three weeks ago, there was a conference in Sacramento, which I attended, run by the state education committee which Mr Wickes represents and the state governor. The conference was well attended by public, private and semi-private universities, and colleges across the state, including mine. One of the topics discussed was the declining numbers of applicants to higher level institutes of education. The discussion was facilitated by Mr Edward Prestbury, chair of the state education committee, and on the board of many of the universities and colleges in this state, including the Marshall Social Institute of Education.

"Roger Sewell, a journalist from the *Northern California Chronicle*, asked an audience question and had clearly done his research, because he made reference to several oral accounts, and cited statistics which indicated that over the course of the previous five-year period, literacy, numeracy and return to work rates had climbed steadily in the catchment area of Endeavour. Mr Sewell had spoken to many teachers and schools in this county who confirmed the statistics, as they had seen the outcome for themselves and heard similar reports from others. Then Mr Sewell asked Mr Prestbury if he was grateful to the work of Endeavour in making learning services more accessible, and more affordable, or if he was in any way concerned about having a strong competitor who was doing more for education than all of the universities put together."

John asked, "What did Mr Prestbury say?"

She replied, "That he had no comment."

He asked, "I see. Why were you and Mr Wickes sent here to see us today?"

Mr Wickes spoke and said, "Mr Cooper, we were not sent here by anyone. From the panel of members on the state education committee, Ms Green and I were nominated, and were elected to come here to make the incentive and acquisition proposal to Endeavour."

John looked around the table and said, "Thank you, Mr Wickes, Ms Green, for your cooperation. I have no further questions. Ms Rochford, is there anything you would like to add?"

Charlie replied, "As Mr Cooper stated, thank you, Ms Green, and Mr Wickes, for your cooperation in providing us with more information about the reasons for your visit. The board of Endeavour is unanimous in our decision against your proposal, but as a matter of courtesy, I, as chief executive of this company, would like to show you the Endeavour Training Academy, as I see you out to the front door of Endeavour."

"That is very generous of you, Ms Rochford. I look forward to seeing what the fuss is about," Ms Green said.

Charlie stood, and she said, "Very well, Ms Green, Mr Wickes, if you would like to follow me."

The three of them left the conference room and returned back down the stairs, where in the lobby, Charlie led them through the double doors into the ground floor academy room.

Charlie said, "Welcome to the Endeavour Academy."

As they both took in the expansive open plan room, the circular clusters and kitchen stations at the back, Mr Wickes looked plainly confused, whereas Ms Green looked around in surprise. They saw the hustle and bustle of a vast room that was full of people, yet the sound from whom was barely audible. They continued to look around, puzzling at the sight before them, then at each other, and finally toward Charlie as they turned away to leave, unable to fully grasp what they had seen, as she led them out the double doors and to the front door of the academy.

As he handed her his badge, Mr Wickes kept mumbling to himself, "I do not understand."

Ms Green, handing her badge over to Charlie, said, "Thank

you, Ms Rochford, I do understand, and this is most certainly not a school nor a trade school."

Charlie smiled and answered, "No, Ms Green, it is not."

CHAPTER THIRTEEN - LONG SIGHT

As Charlie walked back into the room, she kissed the top of Michael's head as she sat down beside him, looked at him reassuringly and then around at the team and said, "That was an experience which required patience and resilience, but it was very helpful."

"It was very helpful indeed. I am going to be very busy for a while," Louisa commented.

Amy smiled and said, "Louisa, I suspect we will all be busy for a while preparing for the fallout, and from what I expect is only the beginning of a storm."

David said, "You are right, Amy, that was only the beginning."

Directing his attention to his wife, David said, "My love, you can breathe now. Apart from the events of that meeting, we have just confirmed important aspects of the work we are doing with Sai. We have evidence that Sai has been trained and tested exceptionally well in how it evaluates, manages, and handles cyber risks, external factor monitoring, quarantining, threats as well as backup and alert handling. The spike was quickly and accurately detected; Sai took precise, precursive steps to monitor, analyse and heighten security measures without our intervention, and the possible connection between the website activity and online chatter was brought to our attention, and faster than it would have taken us to spot the anomaly ourselves, plus Sai detected that the chatter did point back to a source in Sacramento, but we couldn't figure out what the connection was. That was a blank in our knowledge, but even so, Sai did precisely what we have designed, and trained it to do."

Jane smiled at her husband, and said, "I needed to hear that."

Charlie added, "Jane, David is right. We had predicted that something like this could happen and had taken steps to prepare for it. That it has happened and though the activity detected was not on a global scale, the actionable insights and intelligence we have gained from it are nonetheless invaluable. Jane, the true value of Sai is only just emerging, and the investment of our time, resources, and our own knowledge into enhancing and building upon Sai has yet again delivered a return, and if I am not mistaken, we are not far from our objective either."

Jane smiled at Charlie and said, "We are not far away at all."

Sam, who had moved to sit by Peggy, his arm around her shoulder, was thinking about the meeting, while listening to everyone's comments, the latter part of which he smiled at and said, "Jane, Charlie, I have a bet on with Devon, John, David, and Michael about Sai, *'how far away is not far away'* is the name of the bet. We might have got carried away with our estimates. He added openly, "Speaking of getting carried away… it wasn't until that meeting but I… I had almost forgotten the world which exists outside of the bustling, thriving place that we know and love as Endeavour."

Michael nodded, curled his fingers around Charlie's hand, and said, "Sam, it reminded me of many of my days spent at the bank. I do not miss those days, with some beautiful exceptions of course," as he tightened his fingers around his wife's hand.

John said, "It reminded me of my days as a lieutenant and, David, of those truly horrible days that I spent looking for a job. I do not miss those days either, but they have taught me well. I will say that it is a very good job that it is me sitting here and not Annie, because she would have slapped Mr Wickes, and she wouldn't even hurt a fly."

Andrea laughed and said, "Annie would have been right, John. I found myself sitting on my hands, and Sam, I know what you mean, there is a simple luxury to Endeavour. By the look on Peggy's face, I gather she is already planning a book about it too."

Peggy smiled and said, "There are plenty of stories yet to be written about Endeavour, and I look forward to the wonderful process of writing each and every one of them. For now, though, back to the reason we are still sitting here. What have we learned?"

Charlie answered and said, "Firstly, Peggy, I love you for everything that you write, and for all that you are, and getting us back to the point. Secondly, I am proud of you all, I want to thank you all because I know that was not easy to sit through. Thirdly, I would like to arrange something for Sara, I don't know what yet, so I welcome all ideas because her swift, decisive actions were truly exceptional today, and bought us time to coordinate and prepare, and though I don't think we will need to worry about Ms Green, Mr Wickes and whoever is actually behind this are a different story."

John said, "Sara is like another daughter to Annie and I, and I am always proud of her, but particularly today. As for what to arrange for her, Charlie, might I suggest finding a way for her to spend time with Andrew?"

Michael said, "That's a great idea John. I am quite sure that Andrew would enjoy that as I've seen the way he looks at her but he is too shy to do anything about it like ask her out."

Jane added happily, "Ooh… yes, I've noticed that too between Andrew and Sara, so yes that's a great idea."

Charlie said with delight, "It could only ever be this wonderful group, the board of Endeavour, after having one of the most difficult and challenging of meetings, that we find ourselves talking about the joyful possibility of a budding love in our midst. Sam, you were right when you said that you had almost forgotten the world that exists outside of Endeavour. I do not lose sight of my love for my own life, or my enjoyment of it, but sometimes I also forget that not everyone shares a similar, or indeed any, love of their own life. To me, it is that love of life which provides the harmonious, uplifting and yes, the truly luxurious atmosphere which we enjoy within Endeavour. An atmosphere which has been created naturally, simply by us being ourselves and running a company in our own way. It is not strange that we might forget from time to time, because thriving, enjoying, and loving our own lives is the only way we know, and is fundamental to who we, as individuals, are.

Michael reached over and proudly kissed his wife just as she had finished speaking, and said, "Charlie Rochford Weston, do you know that you have a beautiful habit of saying the most wonderful of statements just when I need to hear them? I fall in love with you and myself every time I hear them, so that is a lot of falling and a whole lot of love too."

Jane said, "Michael, you are not alone in that. Charlie, I love you too."

Sam added, "Charlie, I love you three, and Peggy, I know four."

There were similar chimes of love from around the room, the pleasure each derived from it powerful and empowering. John, who was more than aware of how different a place Endeavour was as a place to work, thought to himself that this was still an entirely new experience and a day he would not forget as long as he lived. He felt immensely proud of himself, and couldn't wait to tell Annie, who he imagined would say why it had taken him so long to see and feel it.

Charlie, her blue eyes sparkling with joy, said, "Okay, so we have established we are a wonderful company of individuals who thrive on life and love. We have also established that we will find a way of arranging for Sara and Andrew to spend time together. Now returning to business and going back to Peggy's precise question, what have we learned from our meeting today?"

Andrea began and said, "In my experience of consulting, and particularly with public sector clients, the apparent lack of research and due diligence about Endeavour was unusual, even for a state agency or state committee, though I acknowledge that budget constraints and time could well have been factors. It is also odd that an appointment was not scheduled in advance, and that more than one meeting was not requested. I also question the claim by Mr Wickes that there had been a committee nomination and election process on who to send, rather than just sending legal and finance representatives who could have handled the whole proposition. This leads me to find that on the whole, the acquisition proposal was not a serious one. Whoever sent Mr Wickes and Ms Green here is not thinking clearly, and the event seems panicked. I was not able to gauge Mr Wickes, but I sensed Ms Green came here more out of sheer curiosity."

Charlie said, "In my experience with similar parties abroad, I agree with you Andrea, the lack of due diligence was odd to me too. Given the absence of a formal proposal, or financials and even basic researched information about Endeavour on the part of the state education committee and the as yet unseen actors involved, I find that the proposal to acquire an equity stake is not an immediate cause for concern but our rejection of it, most certainly is. The perceived competitive threat which the journalist, Mr Sewell, posed at the conference, whether accurate or not, was I find the motivator for the visit. Again, I agree with you Andrea, it suggests a degree of panic. Thinking the situation through, ignoring the non-disclosure agreement, as breaching it would be expensive for the state or these unknown actors. The likeliest course of action would be an attempt to draw us out, force us to disclose information about Endeavour, which would then be used against us. Evaluating many probable pathways, I speculate that we would most likely be targeted with allegations that we are anti-competitive, operating a monopoly, and that Endeavour does receive some form of state or federal funding, which will require us to publish financial information."

Sam said, "Asking for a twenty-percent stake in Endeavour, without a formal proposal, rationale or some form of business case is, I agree, unheard of, even for the state or state agency. It is possible, however, that the people who orchestrated this were being very lazy, and wanted us to do the work for them, but I suspect it is more a case of someone thinking that we can be bullied into submission. That we rightfully rejected the acquisition proposal will accelerate any campaign against Endeavour, because the people in charge will not be happy. We are a wholly owned private company, but every attempt will be made to ignore our rights as a private company.

"Devon, in our due diligence screening of our customers in the trade centre, I don't recall seeing references to state or federal subsidy or grant recipients, not that would we prohibit customers who do receive benefits of some kind from trading with us, but could this be a way of alleging that we are indirectly receiving state or federal funding? There may well be an attempt to apply pressure on us, by way of audit or investigation to force us to comply with disclosure rules, thus it merits us at least looking at the definition of indirect payments and preparing accordingly.

"Also, Charlie, lest I should forget, on the opportunity you spotted, looking at the university's financial records, it merits further assessment. We have looked at expanding, we have the capital to do it, and as we proved from the sandbox to here, what we do at Endeavour transfers and scales, and I would like to explore it further."

"Thanks, Sam, we can do our own research, and explore from there," Charlie said.

Devon said, "Sam, on indirect payments, what constitutes a payment appears to be vague, which is not surprising given that most companies do want to make public debt offerings available to the stock market, so a definition has not been needed. As the way Endeavour is structured and funded is an exception, and until or unless the definition is clarified, there is no legal basis to challenge us on it. Though if someone had the time and resources, embroiling us in a lengthy court battle could, I imagine, be seen as worthwhile for some, even if it was for no other reason than to make us look uncooperative, argumentative, and just another big bad company. On that Sewell journalist we heard mentioned, the *Chronicle* published an article written by him after the conference which does mention Endeavour, but it is the picture that came with it, which I am more interested in. I have shared a link, take a look at it."

Jane brought the link to the article up on the big screen monitor in the conference room, and the picture which accompanied the article, credited to Roger Sewell, showed two men, Mr Shawn Trammel, and Mr Edward Prestbury.

Amy was the first to express her thoughts and said, "A picture is not always a reliable artefact because it cannot describe the context of why it was taken, or the circumstances which led up to it, however, based upon the expression, pose and stance of these two men, I would say Mr Prestbury is a deer caught in headlights, Mr Trammel is an opportunist, and I would go so far as saying they know each other but do not like each other. Mr Prestbury may be one to watch but I dare say Mr Trammel is the dangerous one."

John said, "I agree with you, Amy. A gut feeling is not evidence, nor is a picture, but this one leaves me with a really bad feeling, and that is coming from someone who has seen truly vile crime scene photographs before. We cannot waste time trying to predict or pre-empt what either of these two are capable of, but further information about both of these characters will, I suspect, serve us well. If Endeavour is going to be collateral damage, time spent armouring our hull will not be wasted effort."

Charlie said, "Let's get on it, John."

Michael was thinking out loud as he said, "I recognise that Trammel guy from somewhere, but I cannot place where."

Sam answered, "I can help with that, Michael. Do you

remember the relaunch of that investment bank which you and I were invited to, many years ago, while we both worked at the bank? Overnight at a black-tie men's only event? They poached lots of people from the bank, and every other bank on the west coast?"

"Oh, yes, I remember now, Sam! Is he the guy who couldn't stop telling everyone how wealthy he was and that it was the investment bank which made it so?"

"That's him," Sam replied, and added, "In the five minutes we spent at the launch, we realised it was dodgy as anything and got out of there."

"I heard so many stories about that bank afterwards," Michael commented.

"Likewise," Sam said.

"Sam, you up for some digging around in the dirt?" Michael asked.

"I thought you would never ask," Sam answered.

"John, two investigative assistants with you on this one," Michael said.

"Welcome aboard, Michael, Sam," John replied.

Louisa said, "Looking at this entire situation, and the information available to us from a fifty-thousand feet view, I do not see any reason why we would need or want to issue any form of public reaction to the online chatter at this time. Our customers here at the academy and in the trade centre, and the people working with Endeavour operations are already loyal, and I am confident that we here in this room can withstand negative press, but I think it would be wise and time well spent to brace ourselves, our suppliers, and our customers for it anyway. We might not need to do anything but that shouldn't stop us from preparing for the possibility."

Charlie said, "I agree, Louisa. We don't want to cause unnecessary alarm, but being proactive instead of reactive here is exactly how we will protect our business, our people, our customers, and theirs. Can you work with Amy, Peggy, and Andrea on internal messaging and how to go about releasing it? We have our Endeavour town hall coming up so it would be useful to use that as a forum. I will talk to Mr Denver; he and I made an agreement and I do owe him more time on his trade stand which will put me very happily in the middle of all the traders there."

She summarised and said, "So what we have learned today is that: Sai accurately detected external noise; that noise was caused by an assertion from a journalist that Endeavour is seen as competition to the mainstream education system in this local area; that report of competition was not enough to be seen as a threat but 'something' happened afterwards which caused people to panic, and the something is likely to be linked to the two men in that photograph. If we had accepted the proposal today, that would have caused more noise, and that we have rejected it will cause a backlash and even more noise. That Mr Wickes and Ms Green showed up today, unannounced, unprepared, and uninformed, suggests a partnership or acquisition was not the aim, and finding out if we really are competition, or really are of benefit to the local community was also not the aim. We are not in competition with schools, but if we are portrayed as being a competitive threat and someone acts, or claims to want to do something about it, then that suggests a political agenda, and a sinister one. If educators, and the institutions they belong to, no longer see their value, and are worried about declining revenues and falling admissions yet are ignoring their dilemma and the measures they could be taking to fix the problems, then those entities will see us as competition, without caring or trying to understand why, or who we are, or what it is that we do.

"The real threat here is the person who thinks that in order to get ahead, it is perfectly acceptable to create fear, to whip up a frenzy which pits two parties against each other to fight a battle, using a twisted, corrupted narrative as the reason, in the hope that no one thinks or examines the cause or the reason, and will then remain intentionally blind to the consequences or outcome. Such a threat is not new to us by any means, but it has a new form which we do need to understand, and all the while knowing that there will be no avoiding it. Endeavour is built on strong foundations; we may take some damage, but it will be surface level because I, indeed we, know our business inside and out, every single piece of it, we know our value, and that value, we know, is worth protecting."

CHAPTER FOURTEEN - OVERSIGHT

"What do you mean they rejected it, Mr Wickes?" Edward Prestbury shouted, his face red with temper as he suddenly stood up from his chair behind his oversized, cluttered desk, his large stout figure, poured into an undersized shabby suit, which seemed to prevent any kind of natural movement, and added to his anger.

Quite used to his outbursts and tantrums, Kathleen Green pulled an embossed white envelope from her handbag, which she handed to him and said, "Sit down, Edward, before you have a heart attack, and when you have a moment, please read this."

He briefly remembered Shawn Trammel and he pleaded desperately, "There must be something you can do, Kathleen?"

She said irritably, "There isn't, Edward. Please open the envelope I gave you and read the contents."

Ignoring her, and still wondering what he could possibly tell Trammel, he said, "This is not going to look good for me. I have a reputation to uphold, people look to me for answers, don't they?"

Terry lied and said, "People do look to you for answers, Edward, don't you worry about that."

Edward calmed slightly and sat down, his bulbous fingers groping the envelope in his hand. Even though he had no idea what it contained, he was afraid to open it because having seen the contents, he would not be able to unsee them. Instead, he elected to ignore the envelope and the problem it contained and asked Kathleen, a woman he despised, and Terry, a coward of a man he hated the sight of, for their ideas on how to fix the more pressing problem at hand.

His calm short lived as Terry handed him the signed indemnity non-disclosure agreement, even though he and his legal advisor buddy Harry Downes had told them to expect one and that they had authorisation to sign it. Edward picked up the phone, dialled a number, and when it was answered, he said, "I don't care where you are, Harry, you need to get to my office, there is a non-disclosure... What? Five minutes? Okay, right."

Kathleen directed a glare at Edward and said, "Edward, as it seems you don't want to open that envelope, will I make it easier for you and instead tell you what it contains?"

"Do we have to do this now, Kathleen, we have other more important things to worry about?"

"You may have, Edward, I do not. I quit."

"What? You can't quit! I will not allow you to quit," he appealed furiously, standing up again, his frame leaning over the desk.

"It is already done."

"But what about the university, you cannot just desert your post?"

"What about the university, Edward? It will be bankrupt soon and there is nothing that can be done for it now."

He screamed, "You backstabbing, horrid, ugly witch! Did you know about this, Terry? How dare you do this to me?"

When Harry appeared a few seconds later at Edward's door he said, "Edward, shut up, and sit down, unless you want another lawsuit on your hands."

He entered without saying another word and put out his hand waiting for the non-disclosure agreement to be handed to him. He read through it, and when he got to the fixed compensation clause, he did a double take and said, "Edward, whoever wrote this document is a savvy legal genius, and they have properly screwed us over. Is this the only copy of this agreement Terry?"

"No, they emailed a copy of this and the waiver, to Kathleen and I," Terry mumbled.

"Then there is a trail which we cannot do anything about. Kathleen, Terry, do not disclose a word of the conversation you had with the board of Endeavour to Edward, unless you and the state are able to pay the stated compensation for the breach, and there is no possible defence against Edward's big mouth. And, Kathleen, don't think for a second that just because you have quit, that this non-disclosure agreement doesn't apply to you, it does and for the next ten years."

"But this is criminal, Harry, those righteous, smug bastards cannot get away with this. Who do they think they are?" Edward implored.

"Is this why you are quitting Kathy?" Terry asked.

"No, Terry. It is not," she replied.

"Then, for god's sake, why?" he queried.

"Because, Terry, everything, and I mean everything that I heard those people at Endeavour say yesterday was correct, we…no, I… have been living in a state of pretence, of denial, telling myself that the university will be okay, that it will survive without doing anything whatsoever to actually ensure that it will be okay, or survive, other than rely on public funds. I know and understand the battle which that police lieutenant said he fought but eventually realised he could not win. I cannot win either so I am going to stop fighting," she said, as she picked up her handbag, stood up, went to the door, opened it and left.

"She'll be back, she has nowhere else to go," Edward said, doubting his own words.

"She won't, Edward," Harry said.

"Harry, what can we do about this non-disclosure agreement? Can we overturn it?"

"It would cost us a lot of money and cause a lot of trouble for you, for me, Trammel and the governor."

"What can we do then?" he pleaded.

As if talking to himself, Terry said aloud, "We cannot let our teachers or our institutions suffer. If we can't talk about those vile people at Endeavour, then the answer is to get them out in the open, and by whatever means necessary."

"We must protect our institutions, and our communities," Edward said, for want of something to say, not grasping the thread of Terry's statement.

"How would we do that, Wickes?" Harry asked.

Terry, delighted to have someone like Harry take an interest in him, said with a spiteful, vindictive tone, "Throw them to the media. Expose them."

"Clever thinking, Terry," Harry said.

"I like your thinking, Terry," Edward said, eventually catching on.

"Harry and I have a lunch meeting with Trammel, will you join us, Terry? He will enjoy hearing your plan, he is a powerful man and needs someone who can make things happen quickly," Edward said, silently thrilled to have someone he hated even more than Trammel, and Downes who he could use as a go between.

"Really, Edward, do you think he will want to hear from me?" Terry asked.

"You are a powerful man on the state education committee. Of course, he will want to hear from you," Edward lied.

CHAPTER FIFTEEN - FORESIGHT

"I need to get more stock from my van out the back. Sam, can you give Charlie a hand on my stall if it gets too busy, please?" Robert Denver called to Sam who was standing, chatting with Michael at his artwork stand nearby.

"Of course, Robert, Charlie and I will hold the fort," he replied.

Robert grinned and said as he walked away from them, "Thanks, Sam, and don't forget Charlie is the boss, she knows what to do, listen to her."

"She most certainly is, she does, I do, and I wouldn't have it any other way," he proclaimed with delight as he stepped behind the counter with Charlie, and though she was busy with a customer, he noticed her glance at him briefly and wink.

He took in the three-sixty-degree view of the trade centre from Robert's stand. He could see the entrance, and as he turned could see many of the other trader stands, lined up in neat rows around the massive room. Raising his head, he could see the full to capacity office spaces around the periphery of the first floor, and in the middle, the staircase to the upper floors which held more office space. When Charlie was finished with her customer, he said, "Charlie, Michael, I have travelled to many beautiful places all over the world but aside from being by my wife's side, this... here... is, I am sure, my favourite place of all."

Michael, who had been renting the stall next to Robert's for months as a place to sell his smaller pieces of artwork and sketches from, also found himself thrilled by the vibrant, colourful atmosphere of the trade centre and said, "Sam, yes, I know precisely what you mean. When I first started selling from here, I thought it was like the trading floor of the stock exchange, but I discarded that notion because to me, there is something far more industrious, productive, honest, and real about this place, so much so that it has inspired a whole new collection of my work. Plus of course, when my beautiful darling wife is here, it adds even more sparkle and energy to the atmosphere."

Richard Dagnam, a spritely, lean, friendly, sixty-nine-year-old farmer who had a meat and dairy stall on the other side of Mr Denver chimed in, and said, "Your young man Michael, right there, is absolutely correct about that. You, Charlie, add a contagious energy to the atmosphere as soon as you arrive. We all notice it; we talk about it often. We notice it with both of you too, Sam and Michael, but Charlie is, by far, more beautiful than either of you. I have been here from day one and I've traded from lots of places over the years, none of which compare to this one, so I do know what I'm talking about."

"Thank you for saying that, Richard, and I am all the more grateful that you are here too because you have kept Peggy and I in plentiful supply of steaks and produce. The very thought of what you may have in stock is a magnet to bring me here, so you are worth your weight in gold to me too," Sam said as he smiled broadly.

"Aw shucks, thanks Sam!" Richard smiled and continued, "Don't be expecting a discount though, Peggy and Charlie get the discounts, you do not. They are much better looking and two of my favourite women."

Sam laughed and said in exchange, "That they very much are, Richard, and two of my favourite women too."

Charlie laughed as she tracked the conversation and as she finished dealing with the next customer, said, "You are very kind Richard, and a solid businessman with a lot of experience, so I trust your feedback about this place. Sam, I know what you mean too. This place is, to me at least, the powerful beating heart of Endeavour. I see it as the physical place which demonstrates how every part of our business is supplying this one, and this is supplying every part of our business. Plus being here is the very forefront of our business, and my favourite part of working is being upfront with customers, and it is more important than ever to me these days."

Michael looked protectively at his wife as she spoke the last few words; it was an admission from her, and he understood its precise meaning. Sam understood it too, as he briefly glanced at Charlie, then looked knowingly at Michael.

They, and indeed everyone working with Endeavour, had become increasingly protective of her, because in the months following the visit by Mr Wickes and Ms Green to Endeavour, Charlie had been the target of a relentless series of vicious media campaigns. It seemed that everything that she had ever said publicly, at conferences or talks, and in interviews on radio, with newspapers or magazines, had been twisted so much and so far out of context, that there was no resemblance between what she was alleged to have said, and what she had actually said as evidenced by the original record. She had been called every name and term under the sun, a money grabbing slave driver, a dictator, a greedy capitalist, a foreigner with no right to be in the country, a parasite who used people to run her company for her. The list was endless and the goal of which was to portray her as nothing else but pure evil.

Charlie ignored the frenzy because what she heard, from these nameless, faceless people, was just empty noise. She had, a very long time ago, freed herself of the ties to the way of thinking which said that living her own life was a punishable offence, and that she should, by default, bow to and accept as an absolute, the judgement, or opinion of others. She saw no difference between the events now to what she had understood back then, except that, where once she thought the only thing to do was stay quiet because no one understood her, she had since learned that by her saying something, anything about herself in her own defence, to anyone who did not truly know her, would amount to her apologising for her own life, and asking others for forgiveness for being herself. Her life and how she lived it, was not a crime, and she had no desire to permit those who would say otherwise, without any evidence of it being so, to penetrate her thoughts, or affect her wellbeing, and interfere with her own outlook on life.

Furthermore, she ignored the noise because despite the onslaught of public interest in the company and in her, the business was growing, and their growth trajectory showed no signs of slowing down. In its entire form, Endeavour, including the sandbox, was now over seven years old, and in that time, the business had grown steadily. In the past year alone, they had tripled their after-tax profit, from fifteen-million dollars the year before, and were on track to do the same in the next. The clients that Charlie brought with her from her previous business into Endeavour had been retained; they had added, over the years, multiple new clients from across the country and overseas to their portfolio, and in the last two quarters alone, had added a record number of new clients. All four floors of Endeavour Academy were operating at capacity. The office spaces they rented out on the upper floors of the Endeavour Enterprise and Trade Centre were full, as were each of the stalls in the trading hall, day in day out. Jane, David, and Louisa were working on a programme, powered by Sai, which would expand their company services online and potentially into new locations. Charlie, Sam, Andrea, and Devon, with Michael as a special consultant, were working with several of their largest clients, on an extraordinary plan of action. Endeavour was truly flourishing, and the area surrounding them was developing too; more businesses and companies had moved in and had set up shop.

Charlie often thought of the email which she, Sam and Devon had received from the office of Mr John Garrett, the chief executive of a local supermarket chain who had complained to her that Endeavour was taking their business. Quite amused by the email, she had arranged a meeting with Mr Garrett during which she pointed out to him that the nearest store to Endeavour was five miles away, and if he really wanted to stop her company taking business from him, then a solution might be to setup a shop closer to Endeavour. Mr Garrett had laughed when Charlie suggested it, because he said that none of his own executives had thought of that as a solution, and that he wished she was part of his executive team. She had laughed and told him that she did not need to be on his team, but that if he wanted to utilise the services of Endeavour, that he and his company were free to do so. They had become firm friends, finding they had much in common. Both were advocates for a free market, the vital role to any business of healthy competition, and above all that competition was nothing to be afraid of to any company who knew its business.

Endeavour knew its business, and without fail at their board meetings, the reason for it came up, that being that they were able to work in the business themselves, and not be tied up in endless, pointless meetings about meetings every day.

They often wondered why they had built their own offices on the top floor of Endeavour Headquarters because they so rarely used them. It was David, in their most recent board meeting, who had pointed out that it was not important that they rarely used their offices; what was important, was that they had constructed a workplace where they were free to choose where to spend their time in their own business. Even with the barrage of vile, detestable campaigns targeted at Charlie and the company, that none of them were hiding away, and were still out in the forefront of the business, meant that they had a direct finger on the pulse of what was actually happening, in, across, and outside the business, first hand and in real time.

Charlie carefully considered David's statement during that meeting and thought of how she loved coaching at the academy, and thrived on the induction courses that she delivered for the people who would be working within the company. She was the chief of Endeavour, and if those individuals had come to them through the academy, or not, it was her responsibility to meet and connect with them, to know them and they know her in a personal and meaningful way. She also thought of how she enjoyed her time with Jane in the tech lab, and with Robyn in the materials lab, but her favourite part of Endeavour was the trade centre, and it was where she spent the majority of her day. She loved watching Michael on his stand near Robert's; she thought of how he and his work were once hidden away from the public, and there he now was, revelling in the experience of being right in the middle of a bustling trading place, meeting the very people who bought his work. Charlie was empowered by seeing the businesses around her growing and developing under the roof of Endeavour, and she felt right at home.

She had felt the wise accuracy of David's words, and told him so by saying, "David, it matters all the more, because it demonstrates to me, the precise mechanics of how, by each of us working within Endeavour, we understand and act on our own personal responsibility, our accountability to ourselves and our role; we are equipped to be able to get things wrong, to make mistakes, to make changes, to make decisions, and we know who needs to be informed, consulted and when. The freedom we have nurtured for ourselves extends to others, in those people who have left Endeavour to go on and set up their own businesses, or pursue other roles and interests, and those who we have seen leave Endeavour to join the staff of other employers but have most often come back to Endeavour."

As much as Charlie had tried over the past several months to reassure Michael, and Sam and everyone, and had tried to encourage them all not to give any mind time or attention, to the ridiculous campaigns over which they had no control, they were all worried for her anyway, none more so than Mr Denver and the traders in the centre, who genuinely loved, admired and respected her, as much as she did them.

Charlie, who had just sold the last remaining bunch of carrots to a customer, asked, "Sam, Michael, Richard, you are all taller than I am, can you see Robert around here somewhere? I know he likes to chat to people but when his stall is low on produce, he knows which is more important. He has been gone a long time, so I am curious about where he is."

Sam replied, "I have just sold the last bag of potatoes and I am wondering the same thing," as he pulled his phone out of his pocket and logged onto the security feed around the trade centre.

"Can you hold the fort, Sam? I will go check on him," she said.

"There is no need, I know where he is, he is talking to someone. Stay where you are, Michael and I will go," Sam said quickly, sending a direct message on his phone to Michael as he said it.

Michael read the message from Sam, followed the link to the feed and saw who Robert was talking to and said, "Yes, Sam and I will go in a minute or two."

"Michael, Sam, what in the world are you two up to? Is there something you are not telling me?" Charlie asked.

"Yes, there is something we are not telling you but there is nothing to say, my darling, until we know more," Michael replied.

Sam and Michael, still monitoring the feed, watched Robert hand two large boxes of produce to the person he was speaking to, and then as he picked up another box himself, they began walking back to the door of the centre. Michael and Sam both looked up from their phones toward the door, where they spotted Robert trailed by a young man, in his late twenties, laden down with produce, both heading in the direction of the stall. Michael said, "Charlie, it seems we have a visitor."

As Charlie followed their line of sight, she saw Robert, and she recognised the young man who walked a few steps behind Robert and replied, "So we do, and I wonder why it has taken him so long?"

Robert looked apologetically at Charlie first and winked, and then did the same toward Sam and Michael. He nodded in the direction of Richard Dagnam and subtly shook his head. He said nothing as he placed the box, he was carrying on the counter in front of her, and taking the other two boxes from the man, he placed them on the counter in front of Sam who stood right beside her.

While Sam and Michael looked confused, Charlie knew Robert so well that she had immediately understood that the wink and then his silence was a cue from him. Taking his cue, she nudged Sam with her elbow and said, "Thank you, Mr Denver. Sam and I have been very busy since you left, we've nearly sold out of everything, would you like us to restock from these?"

"Of course, I want you to restock from these, I don't pay either of you to stand around idle."

"No, Mr Denver, you do not pay us for that at all. Is there something I can get your friend there?" she said.

"My young creative friend here is one Mr Roger Sewell, a journalist from the *Northern California Chronicle*. Perhaps it is my age and times have changed a lot, but it seems that a yearlong search looking for frogs in a pond full of them would still end up being a story," he answered.

"Is that so?" Sam asked, as he and Michael both observed Mr Sewell with caution.

Mr Sewell was not paying attention to Robert, nor to whom Robert was speaking. Instead, he appeared to be taking in the enormity of the trade centre around him and was already scribbling frantically in the notebook which he had pulled out of his pocket.

Usually, Charlie found anyone who looked around the trade centre with such visible awe, endearing, but less so with the man in front of her. To bring his attention back to her, she said, "You have come a very long way from San Francisco, Mr Sewell. What brings you to San Diego?"

Upon hearing his name and the question posed so confidently,

Roger Sewell directed his attention toward the woman, dressed in smart casual attire as if she had just come from a meeting, yet stood behind the stall counter with a tall man beside her, both unpacking the boxes in front of them. She looked vaguely familiar, but he could not place her face, so replied courteously, "Yes, ma'am, I am here to try to meet the owners of this place and get an interview for a piece I am writing. I've been talking to Mr Denver outside and he told me that I could meet the owners right here."

"I see, Mr Sewell. In which case, how can I help you?" she asked.

"Not the owners of this stand, ma'am, I mean the owners of this centre," he said, confused by her question.

Michael, Sam, Robert, Richard, and other nearby traders who were listening with interest to the exchange, tried their best to suppress their amusement.

"Again, Mr Sewell, how can I help you?" she asked.

"I mean no disrespect, but I don't believe you can," he answered politely, still trying to place her face but when nothing came to him, he gave up trying.

"Is that so? Do you know who the owner of this centre is Mr Sewell?" she asked.

"Yes, a company named Endeavour," he replied.

"You are here to meet a company?" she inquired.

"No, madam, I am hoping to meet the people who own the company," he said.

"Mr Sewell, you are a journalist, might I ask what type of article you are writing?" she asked patiently.

Rather confused by the change in her line of questioning, he replied, "An investigative piece about the impact this company has on the local community."

"Do you enjoy investigative journalism, Mr Sewell?" she asked.

"Yes, very much so and I am very good at it, my editor says so," he answered proudly.

"How long have you been a journalist?"

"About a year now as a paid journalist, before that some freelance work here and there."

"Which part of investigative journalism do you enjoy?" she asked.

"Mostly, I enjoy digging up a story and then writing about it. I suppose I like it too as I get to travel, see places, and then expense my travel."

"What have you learned or researched about this company and the local community?" she asked.

"This is my first-time visiting San Diego, but I have read and written a lot about what this company has done for the community."

"Do you care about the subjects that you write about, Mr Sewell?"

"Not particularly, ma'am, I just really enjoy writing about whatever comes into my head, and then seeing my articles published. I have a very large online following, so I get paid to write to keep my readers and followers happy. My editor says that with my recent performance, I have gathered quite a following in political circles, and if I play my cards right, I might be sent to Washington soon."

"That seems like an interesting career trajectory. Mr Sewell, do you want to be a political correspondent? Do you enjoy politics?" she asked.

"No, I detest politics but if I can make a lot of money at it, then I am more than happy to do it," he said. Keen to change the subject, get back to his article and then take some snaps for his social media feeds, he asked, "What about you, ma'am, do you like working here?"

She stared at him momentarily, as she considered identifying herself to him, and answering the question which to her mind, would have been the first and most obvious one to ask but she thought better of it, instead opted to answer his question, and said, "Yes, Mr Sewell, I thoroughly enjoy working here. Coming to Endeavour every day, being at the very centre of this business, meeting lots of customers, and from time to time selling produce to consumers, is how I love to spend my day. Running a stall, just like a business, is hard work, but I find it incredibly rewarding."

"This doesn't seem very glamorous to me. Don't you want to be more than someone who just sells produce for a living though, ma'am?"

"Mr Sewell, like every trader in this very place, I am far more than someone who just sells produce, or indeed anything, for a living. I am a businesswoman, running a business that I love," she answered.

"Is this stall your business?" he asked.

"No, it is not. This belongs to Mr Denver, but I work here from time to time. I have a business related to this one though, a large one," she said.

"You do? My fans will love to see a young female entrepreneur who has her own business, plus it will also give me a great political angle. Do you mind if I ask you some questions then?" he said.

"By all means," she answered, as she sold a small bag of potatoes to Mrs McGrath, a regular customer to the stall who had been following the exchange, and as Charlie handed Mrs McGrath her change, the old woman leaned in and whispered conspiratorially, "I won't say good luck Charlie. You don't need it, but he most certainly will."

"How long have you been in business?" he asked.

"At this location, approximately five years now, in total, about fifteen years."

"That is impressive for a woman of your age," he commented.

"It is an impressive achievement for either a man or woman, of any age."

"You have an unusual accent; you are not American?" he asked.

"No, Mr Sewell, I was born in Ireland, but now I am an American citizen."

"You are a young female immigrant and entrepreneur, that is even better again. What is the hardest part for a woman setting up and running a business?" he asked, as he scribbled down more notes.

"Setting up, running, growing, developing and being responsible for a business is a hard challenge for anyone. That I am a woman does not increase or decrease my capacity, or ability to do either," she replied.

"As a businesswoman, what inspires you to get out of bed in the morning?" he asked.

"Life does, and what motivates me to get out of bed is the wonder about the yet to be discovered knowledge of what the day will bring," she answered plainly.

"That is not a very businesswoman-like answer," he said.

"Let me restate it for you then. By discovering and using my knowledge, I earn and gain a profit. My wealth is what I accumulate from applying that discovered knowledge to enhance and improve my life," she said.

"That seems like a very profound response, but it is still not a very businesswoman-like answer," he said.

"What exactly would a businesswoman-like answer sound like to you then, Mr Sewell?"

"That you are in business to make money."

She hesitated for a moment and then said, "I am in business to make money, and specifically to make a profit."

"It must be hard for a businesswoman in this economic climate to make a profit. Are you at least able to make a living from your business?" he asked.

"Mr Sewell, in order for me to answer that, may I ask you a question?"

"Of course, ma'am," he replied.

"When you walked into and through this trade centre, Mr Sewell, may I ask what you observed as you did so, and continue to observe as you look around you now?"

"I noticed the throngs of people, and the hustle and bustle of a thriving marketplace, a wonderful atmosphere of camaraderie in here, the whole of which I must admit surprises me, as I have heard terrible things about the owner of this place so now, I don't know what to believe," he said.

"Does this place of business appear affected by the economic climate you mentioned?"

"It does not, ma'am. Just as I'm speaking to you, I am noticing lots of people buying from you and the other stalls," he said.

"That is very interesting, Mr Sewell, and to answer your original question, yes, I am able to make a living from this place, and from the entire company," she said.

"Good for you, ma'am, that you are clever enough to piggyback off the owner of this company, and make a living at it," he said.

"That is a peculiar thing to compliment a person for. Regardless of which, I do not need to piggyback off the owner of this company, Mr Sewell, I am the owner of this place," she said.

"I know the owner, ma'am. You are much too young, too friendly, open, and straight-forward to be the owner," he said bashfully.

"Do you? Am I? That is quite curious, Mr Sewell, because you say you know the owner, yet I am Charlotte Rochford, chief executive of Endeavour."

"But that is impossible, you look nothing like the photos I have seen of you online," he exclaimed, not quite believing her, even though now that she had said it, she had looked familiar to him at the beginning of their exchange.

"I can assure you; it is not impossible. I am Ms Charlotte Rochford. You are, Mr Sewell, standing in one of my businesses, which is also the business of Mr Walker here, Mr Weston seated over there at his stall and many others. The people in this very building, or in any of the other two Endeavour buildings on this site, can verify my identity if need be."

"You look nothing like how Mr Wickes or Mr Trammel described you either," he said, still not quite believing her and wishing he had put more time into researching her.

She eyed him cautiously at the mention of Mr Trammel and Mr Wickes, and she really wanted to laugh at the ridiculous statement she heard from him, but she remained professional and said, "I have met Mr Wickes. I have not had the opportunity to meet Mr Trammel. I cannot conceive of how either could possibly have described me," she said. She followed up and said, "Mr Sewell, as I understand from this exchange, you came here from San Francisco to meet the owners of Endeavour for the purposes of your article, and now that you have, do you have further questions for me?"

He was thinking of how he could spin this interview with this woman, who was not at all what he had expected, from what he had read online, nor was she hostile, or uncooperative as Mr Wickes had described her, when he had last met him, Harry Downes and Shawn Trammel, in the office of his editor, Philip Whitsop, at the *Chronicle*. He then remembered what they had promised him and said, "Yes, I have some more, Ms Rochford."

Charlie, out of the corner of her eye, noticed the concerned look on Michael's face, and Sam moved ever so slightly closer as if he were her bodyguard. It seemed to her that the usual busy sounds and motion in the trade centre had been muted. Mr Dagnam and Mr Denver stood together as if ready to pounce on Mr Sewell at a moment's notice.

"How do you feel about Mr Trammel running for Congress?" he asked, writing the question in his notepad, and waiting for her response.

"I have learned of Mr Trammel, but I do not know him, and I have no feelings or opinion on the matter of his running for Congress," she replied frankly.

"I feel that you should know Mr Trammel, as he is very popular amongst my readers and fans. He has done great things for businesses across the state and country, he is an avid supporter of women in business, an equal rights and immigration advocate, and he is already doing wonderful things for our teachers, schools, and universities, and I think you should want to meet him," he suggested.

"I see, perhaps you could give me some examples of the great things he has done for businesses in California, Mr Sewell?" she asked.

"I can give you two as my editor has asked me to write about them. Mr Trammel has recently launched a special fund for start-up businesses, from his own personal wealth, partly funded by the state and the federal government, which makes funding available to new entrepreneurs for business development, if their enterprise has proven to be successful in the first three years of their launch. He has also initiated a small-town development campaign, the aim of which is to entice landlords, and commercial property owners, to reduce the rental costs in suburban and rural towns, to make it easier for businesses to set up and trade, and for local residents to shop and buy locally," he said proudly.

Charlie could not help but feel compassion for the young man in front of her. She wondered at what point in his life he had become so eager to please others, that he had become oblivious to thinking about who it was, exactly, that he was looking to please, and why. Granted, she did not know him well but so far, this man seemed to be yet another victim in a game of such malevolent evil, that Charlie really struggled, as she always did, to bear the thought of it. A vile, despicable game being played, by men and women who were either raised, or often at their own convenience, to believe that they were created in the image of a god. Their belief permitted them the right to do whatever they liked, with no consequences to bear, in the name of that god, if they asked forgiveness from that god, no matter how cruel, evil, and morally incomprehensible their act. The only reprimand: a prayer to be recited alone, in silence, to nothing but thin air, with no thought for accountability, or personal responsibility to be taken toward their victims.

She looked over toward Michael, taking in and loving every part of the beautiful sight of him, as his eyes were firmly fixed on Mr Sewell. As he moved his eyes to meet hers, she touched her hips with her hands, and smiled as she saw him laughing at her swibbling motion, which he then returned. She thought of their unique vocabulary, neither a punishment or prayer amongst the words that they had created, nor amongst their actions in their many years together or apart, across thousands of miles, and through thick and thin. She drew strength from him now, collected her thoughts, directed her attention back to Mr Sewell and said, "I would theorise that Mr Trammel will not make it to Congress, Mr Sewell."

"He must make it to Congress, he says he is a man of action, and so far, he has proved it," he declared.

"Do you have any further questions for me, Mr Sewell?" she asked.

"Yes, I do. What do you have to say to the teachers and schools in this community who feel threatened by your company?" he asked.

"Are they threatened, Mr Sewell, or have they seen a remarkable improvement in literacy, numeracy, and increased return to work rates amongst various segments of the population here in the local area?"

"Well, teachers, schools and employers have reported marked improvements, but Mr Trammel and Mr Wickes have formulated a plan to remove competition, in order to protect valuable institutions of education," he answered.

"Is that their plan, Mr Sewell?" she asked, paused briefly, and said, "As I trust you have sufficient information from me, and it has been very insightful conversing with you. If you would please excuse me, I must get back to my work. By all means, please carry on interviewing the people in this centre. Or if you require further information, please contact Louisa Willis, Endeavour's chief of communications, you will find her details on our website." she said politely.

"Thank you, Ms Rochford, but I have one last question. What would you like to say to Mr Trammel when he is here next month?" he asked.

"I was not aware of his planned visit to San Diego, and as I do not know him, nor his agenda, I do not care to say anything to him," she stated simply.

"That is quite peculiar, Ms Rochford, as both Mr Wickes and Mr Trammel gave me the impression that you would already be aware, that you would care, and would be interested in speaking to him," he said with a confused tone, wondering if he had recalled the conversation with Mr Wickes and Mr Trammel properly.

Charlie observed Mr Sewell carefully as she heard the confused tone to his voice. She found herself deeply grateful to him, for inadvertently, in his confusion, giving her a small clue on what Mr Trammel, Mr Wickes and whoever else was involved, might be likely to orchestrate next. She said, "Mr Sewell, that is indeed very peculiar. It seems I may well be speaking to Mr Trammel after all. For now, however, I am very grateful to you. It has been quite an experience to meet you here today and I expect we will be meeting again, very soon."

"Thank you, Ms Rochford. You have been most generous with your time, not at all what I thought you were going to be like. I am deeply sorry that I did not recognise you, but I have learned three valuable lessons as a result today, one being to do better research, another to not judge a book by its cover, and finally not to take what others have said about the book too seriously, unless I have read it myself," he said genuinely.

Charlie looked at him with surprise, as she considered his statement, and their conversation thus far, and with a flicker of growing respect for him, she said gently, "You have indeed learned something valuable, and you have earned the beginning of my respect for doing so, and for admitting it, which is, in itself, an achievement, Mr Sewell."

He looked at her with astonishment as if she had handed him gold when he saw the look of genuine respect toward him on her face. He was quite taken aback by it, but he gathered himself, held out his hand to shake hers, which she took, and then he said, "Ms Rochford, I would like to thank you again, very much so."

Charlie smiled as she watched him walk away, pausing occasionally as he passed by the stalls, on his way towards the door. It seemed to her that he had a spring in his step, and a lightness to him. She hoped she was right, and if so, that it would last and serve him well and then she supposed that she would soon find out.

Bringing her focus back to her immediate surroundings, she first saw Sam beside her, smiling broadly, a look of deep admiration and fondness toward her on his face. Then she saw Michael coming toward her, walking behind the counter, as he said, "Charlie Rochford Weston, you are, my sweet, kind, and beautiful darling, the most incredible woman in this world. I am the proudest of men to call you my wife, and so I do this for me, for you and for everyone in this entire building, and in this company." To which he proceeded to pull her close to him, and then he kissed her deeply. They both giggled as they heard Sam, Robert, and Richard chorus for them to get a room, followed by a rapturous round of applause as the atmosphere in the trade centre returned to its usual levels. She heard Richard Dagnam say, "You see, I told you, you hear it now, don't you?"

She smiled at Richard and said in reply, "I do."

Robert said, "Charlie, all that media coverage about you has had me and everyone here worried about you for months, and I admit that I couldn't understand why you seemed to be indifferent to it, but when Mr Sewell started talking to me outside, and then I heard that exchange between you both just now, I finally see why you were so steadfast in your judgement that the coverage was nothing to worry about. I will not apologise for worrying about you, but I will apologise for not listening to you."

She looked at Robert and Richard Dagnam in turn, then at Michael who still held her close, then at Sam beside them and said, "I know that you have all been worried, and that is because you love and care deeply, not just about me, but about yourselves and the life you have each worked hard to create, and for that, Robert, there is nothing to apologise for.

"If this entire episode has proven anything, it has demonstrated that there is to my mind, order in chaos, and chaos in order. Chaos is often a convenient tool of distraction; by examining chaos, and putting its components in a hierarchical sequence, this serves as a useful way to identify what is just noise and what the signal to the root of the chaos is. The same is true of order; I have found by examining the most seemingly orderly of processes or activities that they are, quite often, either by accident or design, creating chaos but then working hard to disguise the chaotic outcome. Identifying the patterns of chaos and order is, in my experience, one of the first steps to be taken towards addressing the underlying problems, and then fixing the root. From that conversation with Mr Sewell, and by examining all the events which led up to this, I now know, the root of the chaos targeted at Endeavour is one of politics, and not of a good kind."

She added, "I have been indifferent to the noise up to now because I was more concerned with knowing and identifying the signal: the root cause. I now know it, and I am not worried now because Mr Sewell provided the key to solving the problem, or at least part of it, as best we can. If we thought Endeavour was under attack all along, it wasn't. Though it soon will be because we are seen as a convenient and easy target. We have nothing whatsoever to be concerned by now, and though it is reasonable to expect that we may take some damage, there will be nothing that we cannot recover from because we know who we are, we know our value, we know precisely what it is that we stand for. Now, however, it is time to stand, not as victims, nor for what we have built, nor for who or what we are, but to stand for that which underpins our entire business within Endeavour which we, each of us, have utilised in abundance to get here: our own individual freedom to think and decide who we are, and why, to choose our own path independently, without the use of force, or by us causing harm to another, and no matter what we are told, or who tries to convince us otherwise."

Sam typed on his phone and said, "A wise and accurate assessment to my mind too, Charlie. As we will need to prepare, but I dare not disrupt the sight of you and Michael, I have asked the team to assemble in the HQ boardroom as soon as they can."

"Thank you, Sam," she said.

Michael said, "Go ahead and count me in, I will be there too."

He pulled Charlie even closer to him and whispered in her ear, "When this is done, you and I are going away together for a while. We will both need repairing, you most of all and I will delight in being the repairman."

She smiled at him, her blue eyes sparkling at the prospect, and she whispered back, "There will be much to repair, and I cannot wait to get started. The ultimate reward awaits us both, and so let's begin to claim it."

Michael smiled knowingly at her and toward Sam, he said, "Sam, we have just reached an agreement, when this is done, Charlie and I will be away for a couple of weeks, so if we can plan for that too."

Robert Denver said, "Charlie, I gave you my commitment a long time ago, you can count me in too."

"And me, you may not need a line of defence, Charlie, but you have one anyway," Richard Dagnam added.

Charlie said, "Thank you, gentlemen, your support and multiple lines of defence, I expect will be needed."

Sam nudged Charlie and told her the team would be assembling in the boardroom of Endeavour in twenty minutes, and that he had asked John and Sara to join them too.

As Michael released Charlie from his embrace and went back to his stall to pack it up, Charlie turned to Sam, smiled at him, then hugged him tightly, and said, "Sam, from Michael and I, thank you for being my, our, line of defence. Also, you needed a hug from me too, Sam. Now let's go help Michael and get over to HQ."

He smiled at her, and as they walked across to Michael's stall, he said, "Charlie, you know I did, and thank you from Peggy and I, for being ours."

A few minutes later, they were all packed up and walking to Michael's car, when Michael asked, "How many lines of defence will we be needing, Charlie? Are we talking about lines of those little green figurines like I used to have as a child?"

"I had those too Michael, and what will these lines of little green figurines cost me?" Sam asked good-naturedly.

Charlie laughed at both of them, and said, "We just found our next board meeting activity, playing with little green figurines as we map out our plan for expansion, and an interesting way of evaluating Sai's progress. We do enjoy visual aids." She added, "For now though, we won't be needing little green men. It is less about lines of defence, and more about protecting the epicentre of what Endeavour is standing for. As for the cost, Sam, there will, I surmise, be an attempt to force us to disclose information which is private to Endeavour. That information will then be used against us, and as a way to void the non-disclosure agreement.

"As I see the situation now, there are two different actors at play here. One who does not care at all about who we are, or what we do, and only wants to use us as a pawn in a game. The other is of the mind that subject to who is asking, our own rights as a private company are void, and we should disregard our own rights because it is the will of the requestor. And that we have no right to our own right to say no, and then doing what is needed to protect our own rights, including not having to justify our reason to the party asking. The reaction to which, as we have observed, has been an attempt to goad us into submission. We have remained silent, working away, getting on with our business and our lives. Our silence was met with more and more aggressive and vicious attempts to goad us and when that failed, the vile narrative was directed toward me."

Sam answered, "They are the worst kinds of bullies. I have seen them on the playground, at all levels of business and in my personal life, and as for the cost, the price we will pay if we do nothing will be far higher."

Michael commented, "So have I, time and time again. We know that this has nothing to do with Endeavour, it is more a case of we have something which another wants, but they don't know or understand what the something is, or why they want it, or how to get it themselves without having to do the work needed to get it, but because we have it, they want and need to have it and see the something as theirs without question, not caring if the something gets damaged, or broken, eventually to be discarded to move onto the next something."

Charlie said, "Precisely, and that, my darling, will be the basis for the script."

Both men looked at her with curiosity and Sam asked, "What script?"

As they reached Michael's car, she turned to both of them and summarised a plan of actions and reasons to them. Neither Michael or Sam were strangers to Charlie's way of working, the product of her beautiful mind, and so rarely had cause to question her judgement, but they both looked at her now with a mix of admiration and incredulity. Then Sam said, "I know you are not crazy, Charlie, but that plan sounds a bit crazy. There has to be another way."

She smiled at Sam and replied, "I have wondered that too, but if there is another way, I know exactly where we will find the brilliant minds, combined with ours, who will discover it. We are on the way to meet them now."

Michael said, "Well, my beautiful darling, and Sam, my wonderful friend, hop in, and let's go two minutes that way to discover and try to find a plan that seems less crazy, though often the crazy plans are the best ones. A little sculpture by a lift in London taught me that many years ago."

As Charlie, Michael and Sam walked into the boardroom, they were greeted with a mix of very curious and very excited faces that looked fit to burst. Charlie looked around thoughtfully and said, "I thought we had news for all of you, but it seems you have news for us too, and by the looks of it, something significant has... Jane, David, could it be?"

Jane, beamed with pride, and replied, "You beautiful oracle, Charlie. We thought something was wrong, but we have run tests. It is no longer a could, Charlie, it is an is."

CHAPTER SIXTEEN - BLIND TO ENDEAVOUR

When Roger Sewell left Ms Rochford and the Endeavour Trade Centre, he found himself stuck between the verge of a conflict and a discovery. The conflict was between the work he had to do for his editor to get his article published, and the discovery was that genuine respect is not an easy thing to attain, nor is it easy to understand what genuine respect looks like.

He compared the words, the look and gesture of respect which he had received from Ms Rochford to that which he had received from his editor, his readers, all his online fans, and many others, friends, and family in his life. He observed there was a difference, and that was in what, and how, he thought about himself, when he heard or read the words, saw the looks, and interpreted the gestures. Not only that, he thought, there was a difference between words purely aimed to flatter but had no meaning, versus words, and he supposed questions too, used to articulate a clear and genuine meaning, a clear narrative, and one of substance.

He pondered why it was that he had said to Ms Rochford that he did not care about what he was writing. He considered that he had been trying to figure out for months how to improve himself as a journalist, advance his career and in so doing increase his reader base. Now, he found that his answer was wrong; he was passionate about writing but not what he was writing about or how. He wondered why it had taken him so long to figure that out, but he was pleased that he did, and as he was an investigative journalist, he would ask himself why. He concluded that he had a lot of research, thinking and testing to do, and as soon as he got back to his hotel room by the waterfront, he began to do just that.

Many long hours of research, notes, and emails later, he placed a conference call to his editor, Mr Whitsop. He began the call by requesting approval to remain in San Diego until after

Mr Trammel's visit. To his surprise, approval was granted by Mr Whitsop. Then he reported back on his meeting with Ms Rochford. He outlined his observations and a summary of the article he would write and submit, after Mr Trammel's visit to southern California was concluded. He had observed and listened carefully to what his editor said, the questions asked, and his own responses. For the first time in a long time, Roger Sewell began to feel proud of himself, as he thought about the lessons he was learning, and what he was beginning to understand.

Whitsop smiled in cunning delight at the report he had received from Roger Sewell, and he could not wait to tell Trammel, Downes and Wickes the good news. He imagined the dramatic headlines that would be running for months as a result. He rubbed his hands together with glee as he thought of the small fortune he would make, to add to his existing wealth, amassed over the years by taking large bribes, in exchange for what he called 'pay us to say anything publishing'. A notoriously shrewd gambler, Whitsop whistled to himself as he calculated the odds of his next big bet. It was late but he knew Trammel would pick up the phone and speak to him no matter the hour; he knew what was good for him, and he needed Whitsop. He placed the call, and when it was answered by the sleepy voice of Trammel, he said, "Sewell the fool did his job. The trap is set, next month you get to spring it, Sewell will be there to report on it, and it will get you to Congress."

CHAPTER SEVENTEEN - ROOT OF ENDEAVOUR

The expansive lobby of Endeavour had been transformed with the stage for the Ron Spencer television show, *America Talks Business*, rigged and ready, the reception area heaving with crew, audience and panel guests, journalists, Endeavour clients and staff, chatting and enjoying themselves, whilst catering staff weaved their way through the crowd with platters of delicious canapes, and light refreshments.

Louisa, who had coordinated the occasion with military precision, was in a celebratory mood, but she, like Charlie and the Endeavour team, were calm, collected, and laser focused on the next few hours. There had been many weeks of preparations to get through, the pressure of which had paled in significance to the chain of discoveries that had surfaced for the company.

Charlie, elegantly dressed in a bias cut, charcoal grey, shift dress with black medium high pumps, Michael by her side, had smiled knowingly as she had whispered in his ear that later that night, they would be packing their bags ready to disappear into the sunset for a while. Next to Michael stood Sam, his tall, slender body, dressed in a navy, tailored suit, with Peggy by his side, his fingers intertwined with hers. The four of them were talking quietly on one side of Ron Spencer, with Devon, Amy, Andrea, Jane, and David on the other, chatting to John Garrett and the other panellists, waiting for the nod from Louisa.

Louisa heard her phone ping the arrival of a message, looking at it, she read, 'Trammel to start his press conference in thirty mins.'

She replied, 'Thanks. The show will begin to broadcast in ten mins, at the top of the hour.'

She nodded at the TV crew director, who signalled to Charlie, Michael, Sam, and Ron and said aloud, "Everyone, places please. It is nearly showtime." As the audience and guests took their seats and settled down, silence descended on the run up to the live call. Louisa tapped her phone, and activated the online campaign feed which she, and the team, had compiled over the preceding weeks. She gave Charlie and Sam the thumbs up, took her seat in the audience at the end of the row beside Andrea, who leaned into her and kissed her gently on the cheek.

"Lights please, camera please, sound please, mics please, camera rolling please, audience cue, Ron cue, and panel cue, music cue go... we are going to live in five... four... three... two..." the director called out.

"A very warm welcome to you all, for this very special episode of *America Talks Business*. I am your host Ron Spencer, coming to you live, this evening, from the headquarters of San Diego, California company, Endeavour. For you watching at home, cameraman John Flynn here is ready to do a panoramic shot, and I will narrate so that you get a sense of the magnificent surroundings that we are in. John, when you are ready.

"This wondrous feat of architecture and engineering which you are now seeing on your screens, and the academy and trade centre structures also on this site, were designed and built by local architect Robyn Foster and her twin brother Anthony. The Foster dynamic duo shot to fame when this incredible building was erected over five years ago, in their use of pioneering technology, engineering techniques and materials which has made Endeavour an iconic landmark of the local landscape. Isn't it just magnificent to see? And what you are seeing is only on the inside, the exterior is truly a sight to behold." Ron said as he focused on the camera in front of him.

"Not only are we broadcasting from a truly splendid location, but we are also coming to you from the beating heart of a company, which despite being the subject of much media attention over the last six months, has become the most successful wholly owned private company on the Pacific coast of the United States. Now into its seventh year of trading as Endeavour, the company yielded forty-five million dollars in after tax profit this past year and is set to triple that in the next. A company that is already taking the United States, indeed the world, by storm as you will hear tonight. For now, folks, I have a splendid line up of conversation in store for you, with my panel of guests behind me ready to get into *America Talks Business*,"

Ron said, as he walked to his host seat at the start of the row, and the camera panned to show the full panel.

****

At that precise moment, in a luxury downtown San Diego hotel, Shawn Trammel, his campaign manager Hilda Sykes, Harry Downes, Terry Wickes and Edward Prestbury were assembled in the hotel lobby, walking toward the entrance to the gala dinner event which would be the launch of Trammel's campaign for a seat in Congress. As they crossed the lobby, the banks of television monitors were tuned into *America Talks Business*, the ticker reel, along the bottom, displaying the location as Endeavour, and headlines from the opening segment about the company's history, and after-tax profit returns.

When the camera panned to show the panel composed of Charlie, Sam and four others, Terry Wickes stopped in his tracks and said, "What in the hell is going on? What are those people doing on television?"

"Who?" Prestbury asked.

"Do you always have to be so dim, Edward? Or are you just so good at it, that it comes naturally to you? Terry is talking about the people from the very company that we are intending to expose and destroy tonight," Harry said.

The next camera shot from *America Talks Business* showed the audience, which was full of the most recognisable business leaders, women, and men from the biggest organisations across the country. Harry whistled as he noted who was in the audience. "Now that is one impressive audience, there must be at least a trillion dollars of net worth within it."

Shawn said nonchalantly, "What do we care and why should that stop us? No one watches *America Talks Business* anyway, so no one will see it, and therefore we have nothing to worry about."

"I do enjoy your confidence, Shawn, even though you are just as dim as Edward is, if you really believe what you just said," Harry replied sardonically.

"For heaven's sake, Harry, please shut up. The only reason we are all here is to make a lot of money. We do not care about those people because they cannot stop us now," Shawn replied with a venomous tone.

"Boys, calm yourselves," Hilda scolded as she turned her attention to Trammel and said, "Shawn you will be going on stage in twenty-five minutes, so please for the love of God, stay away from drinking anything beforehand. You need to be clear headed and ready for this.'

She silently hoped he would ignore her advice and then reminded herself that she would not be seeing any campaign through for Shawn Trammel, so it did not matter to her what he did.

****

The camera on the set of *America Talks Business* continued to pan to take in the full panel as Ron Spencer introduced, to rapturous audience applause: Ms Charlotte Rochford, Endeavour CEO; Mr Samuel Walker, Endeavour Treasury; Cheryl Grantham, MD and CEO of AnaePharma, Teddy Samuels, CEO of Symbal Technology, one of California's largest technology companies; Mr John Garrett, CEO of the Broadway Grocery chain; and Rachel Gill, CEO of AviateEngineering, the largest aircraft manufacturer in the United States.

Ron said, "Charlie, Sam, you are our very gracious hosts this evening and I will come back to you both in just a moment. John, great to have you here on our panel, and I look forward to a frank discussion with you too. Firstly though, Cheryl, Rachel, Teddy, you are all frequent guests on *America Talks Business*, so please answer me this. What does a pharma company, a technology company, an aircraft manufacturer, a supermarket chain, and all the other business sectors represented here this evening, have in common?"

Cheryl answered, "Thanks, Ron. It is a true pleasure to be back in this magnificent building once again, and for such a momentous occasion. I will get straight down to business by saying that there are two answers to your question. The first is that we are all, at our core, businesses who make goods and services available for customers to buy. The second answer is Endeavour. This very company is the beating heart of what the businesses represented here tonight, and many others have in common, but which many of us, including my own, had for a long time forgotten.

"And what is that, Cheryl? What has been forgotten?" asked Ron.

"That the only way to be successful in business is to know the precise value of what it is we are doing, why, for whose benefit; that the only party we should be most concerned about are our own customers. By customers, I mean, those who pay a price in exchange for what they receive, and that extends to anyone we have an agreement with, ourselves, the people who work within our organisations, and our end customers. Without understanding the value of what we are providing to our customers, and all along the supply chain, we are failing to take ourselves or our businesses seriously; we are merely playing a game with other people's money, on the chance that anything will do, that customers do not deserve more because they do not know any better, or worse still, they will tell us where we are going wrong, and what to do better.

"AnaePharma, Ron, makes anaesthesia drugs. The party who matters to my business are the patients who receive those drugs before, during or after a surgical procedure. The secondary party who matters to my business are the medical professionals delivering those drugs. The core of my business is to ensure that every product which leaves our labs and manufacturing lines will end up making the lives of the patient easier, pain free, and where possible, get them back to health and wellbeing, safely, quickly, and efficiently. I will openly admit, Ron, that for years my business forgot that, becoming more focused on profit margins, lawsuits, stock prices and what our competition was doing. We ended up tanking, we lost our focus, we lost people because we were not listening to them. In the end, we lost market share, and gained debt. We looked at taking the usual measures of cutting costs, without knowing or even understanding what value we were removing from the business, and the price we would ultimately pay. Instead of facing reality, and questioning our own motives, we listened to the same old stories of an economic slump, just a rough few years; all the while we began playing political games involving blame, with no one accepting responsibility. When I became chief executive, the phrases I heard most often in my boardroom began with we 'should', we 'would' or we 'could' but no solutions, or actions came with them. A 'should' is not going to help or do anything for a patient, or the medical personnel providing care to that patient in the operating room or afterward."

Ron asked, "That is quite a statement you are making on the airwaves. What did you do, Cheryl, to get AnaePharma back to being profitable, and for what, now five years running?"

She answered, "I went looking for help and I found it with Endeavour, oddly enough, because a supplier in Munich, Germany had recommended Ms Rochford to me."

Ron asked, "Cheryl, that was a long way to go for a recommendation and seems like a very straightforward answer. John Garrett, you are the CEO of the Broadway Grocery Markets chain, is Cheryl's answer that straightforward?"

John answered, "Cheryl is right on the money, Ron. In my case, I opened my first grocery store on Broadway almost thirty years ago, and today I am responsible for a company, with a chain of one-hundred stores across the southern part of the state. None of which, however, would be possible were it not for the thousands of people who work across the business and in my stores. Those people are the ones who enable customers to walk through the doors of my stores, to buy from me, and my suppliers. But I found myself, as the years went by, becoming so far removed from those people, from what was happening on the ground in my stores, that I lost sight of my own business and then wondering why my company was barely profitable, and losing market share. Cheryl is right again about hiding behind phrases like economic climate, rules and regulations, rising costs and stiff competition, without checking the facts, evaluating the patterns and then acting in creative and meaningful ways on those facts and patterns. As I say Ron, I lost sight of my own business.

"I recaptured that sight, shortly after I had sent a very petulant complaint to Ms Rochford there, in which I claimed that Endeavour was taking my business from me. The response I got from her was to arrange a meeting and talk about the nature of my complaint as businesspeople, and not as children in a playground behind each other's backs. In the meeting which followed, Charlie pointed out to me that the nearest store to Endeavour was five miles away, and if I really wanted to stop the trade centre taking business from me, as I had claimed it was, then a solution might be to set up a store closer to Endeavour. I laughed when she suggested it, because not a single person on my own executive team, or I, had thought of that as a solution. My initial response to her solution was to claim that it was unfair of her company to have a monopoly on the people who could help my business. Her answer was to ask two questions and I quote them now: 'Why is it that you expect me, or my team, working in positions they enjoy, to give up their jobs, to join yours because you demand it, as a means to be shown or reminded of how to run yours? And do you see that if you need help, you are free to utilise the services of Endeavour, not by petulant demand but by mutual agreement?'

"The lessons I learned, and what I needed reminding of, were many in that meeting, that competition is nothing to be afraid of to any business who actually knows its own business, and that the most honest response within a business which is showing signs of going backwards, is not to assign blame to others or outside causes, but to accept responsibility by admitting that if I don't know something, the only person who can find out is me, and in doing so, to create the type of workplace where a 'let's do this differently' attitude is rewarded, and not trampled or frowned upon."

"I like the way you phrased that John, a 'let's do this differently attitude'. How, may I ask, did you begin to do that?" Ron asked.

"Quite simple really, I began by putting myself in the shoes of the customers who were walking through my doors. I went to my own stores as a shopper, with a list and a shopping cart. I then asked my board members and senior executives to do the same." John replied.

"Well that does seem like a different way of doing things, quite an obvious one too, now that I think about it," Ron commented and then asked, "What did you learn from the process?"

"I learned, Ron, that doing the same thing, in the same way as everyone else, for no tangible, material reason, other than perhaps *'this is the way we have always done it'*, is not a differentiator, and there is no value to me, my business, or to my customers in doing so."

"From what you have said John, and you also Cheryl, it seems to me, there is a pattern emerging here. Rachel Gill, CEO of Aviate Engineering, is this a pattern? Do we have a problem in corporate America?"

She replied, "Yes, Ron, I believe we do have a problem, and it is not just isolated to corporate America. It is a global phenomenon, and is corrupting governments and businesses alike to such an extent that companies and entire economies are throttling their own growth. I have detected, and observed it within Aviate, across my supply chain and within the airlines, across the many countries that we supply to."

"Is it a global phenomenon, Rachel? Can you explain why you believe that to be the case?" Ron asked.

Rachel said, "By all means, Ron. Aviate Engineering has been around for six decades. Our longevity and success has not been achieved by us manufacturing aircraft as cheaply as possible. It has been attained through our passion for research and development into, and then by using, the newest, most innovative emerging materials, parts, tools, and technology that we can source or create ourselves, so that every component, in every craft we produce, is built and engineered with safety, passenger and crew comfort, as well as efficient flying design, longevity and ease of maintenance in mind.

"Once upon a time, I was able to source high quality materials, and I could rely on those materials, and the tools I needed to be transported, imported and delivered on time. Yet, despite the vast improvements we have seen over the last twenty years in global transport and logistics, not only had there been a visible downgrading of what 'quality' and the price of that quality means, it was often the case that the goods I need, did not even leave the supplier's factory, never mind reaching Aviate, on time. When I would ask why, I was met with a variety of answers from procurement, legal or payment delays, customs and excise clearance problems, insurance liability rules, antitrust, to tax liability rules. The list was endless, the length of which increased exponentially country by country."

Ron asked, "They seem like reasonable answers to me, Rachel? Why did you not think so?"

"They did, at first, Ron, seem like reasonable answers to me too, and I was content to give suppliers the benefit of the doubt, however after hearing the same answers, time and time again, and from different suppliers, I began to see a pervasive problem. It is a very easy thing to assign blame to the myriad of rules, and regulations, which businesses have to follow but doing so simply shifts accountability, and ownership, of the underlying problems from one party to the next. This shifting of blame is seen as a handy, catch-all solution but it does not actually change, or do, or achieve, anything, it merely gives way to an exacerbation of the problem by brushing over the cause."

Ron said, "What did you find the cause to be, Rachel?"

"The cause, Ron, is grounded on the sole emphasis given by many business owners and their stakeholders on profit, but not to the identification, or recognition of value, or on what is fundamentally required, in order to produce 'something' of value, which can, firstly, be sold or exchanged for a price, and then at a profit.

"An aircraft, or the phone in your hand, or the television screen you are watching this show on did not just magically appear. This show, for instance is the culmination, the product of the minds of individuals who designed, engineered and built the power plants, the telecommunications infrastructure, those who sourced the raw materials needed to create the hardware, the software, the glass, the plastics, the wiring, the screws, the tools needed to make the camera, the sound equipment, the set, the screen you are watching this on, and the myriad of people who are trained and skilled at operations and delivery. The same is true for an aircraft, a laptop, or a phone, or any object you see around you; this building, for instance, did not just appear out of nowhere. Even with the advances in robotics, artificial intelligence or the most complex of computing technology, it still requires people who can think, innovate, collaborate and produce to actually make, then deliver and operate that something. People had to think first, then work to create it and produce it, each and every part of the 'something' first.

"As for the natural resources, and raw materials which need to be extracted from this planet to make the very things, the modern conveniences, which consumers – I myself being one of them – have come to rely upon, even they have been corrupted by political, environmental and social policies, under the guise of activists and lobbyists who are destroying entire economies, and putting the livelihoods of the people, who live in those economies at risk. Many companies, and governments alike, have become more concerned about what they are seen to be doing, rather than what they are actually doing. By that I mean, chief executives, business owners and leaders taking personal responsibility and accountability for actually producing and for an actual value, which will actually deliver a real, meaningful, and beneficial value to the end customer, consumer, or taxpayer, and all the way through the supply chain.

"To safeguard the future of Aviate, we took extraordinary measures by insourcing, and vertically integrating all of the manufacturing of the parts, components and tools which are needed to build an aircraft. We built a freight fleet, so that we can send our own aircraft, and ships to bring the raw materials we need back to our manufacturing plants, faster and on time. We acquired mines, and mining operations which we run and manage ourselves, so that we could be sure that workers and their children in particular, were not being used as modern slaves. This has been expensive, yes, but our dependency on a corrupt, broken, supply chain which operated on promises, estimates, and poor quality has diminished.

"The win for Aviate is that we are back to full and proper aircraft production, accountable and responsible for every part of the process. We are leveraging technology, tools and processes which have accelerated our manufacturing and distribution chains. We have recruited thousands of exceptional people around the world, who are proud to be doing what they love every day, in a way that they love. I know they are proud because I have met and spoken to each of them myself.

"I, as the chief executive of Aviate, have never been prouder of what we are now achieving and how we are achieving it. I am proud of the value, that I know without question, that we are truly delivering to clients, and above all that the profits we are generating have actually been earned, and to be reinvested back into the business, back into the people, who are, as John and Cheryl said earlier, the fundamental core of why Aviate is now able to produce fleets of aircraft that are safer, easier to operate, maintain, more energy efficient, resulting in more comfort, and a richer flying experience for passengers and crew alike, than many of our previous lines. Aviate went back to basics, by retraining ourselves on where exactly the value truly lies in our business, and yes, the help we needed to do that, was also Endeavour."

"That is yet another powerful statement from a business magnate, Rachel. I think it would be quite apt to rename this episode to *America Talks Business Therapy*," Ron said. Then he asked, "Teddy Samuels, you are another leading industrialist as CEO of Symbal Technology, what are we missing from the equation, is there more to it?"

Teddy replied, "If we take my own business down to brass tacks, Ron, then we may find that there is. Rachel Gill is right about the root of the problem, Ron. Symbal Tech has been around for well over a decade now. I started the company from my garage, from where I nurtured and cared for it, building it from the ground up slowly but surely, creating technology products which, because I had done my research on the market, I knew customers would buy, and they did.

"To scale my business, I hired more people to create more products, thinking that would be the automatic way to sell more, but business is not automatic. To create more products required more raw materials, those materials cost money, there were shipping and import costs and taxes to pay, then there were salaries, wages to pay to all those people, that I needed to create more products. There was rent to pay, more taxes, insurance costs for every possible eventuality and other costs like energy, technology costs, down to coffee supplies in the office canteen. To keep growing, I needed more people to sell, and to find distribution channels. I took out a second mortgage on my home, in order to borrow from the bank, which gave some breathing space, but that added even more pressure.

"The basic rule of any business is that to cover costs, the monetary amount of products sold needs to exceed costs, and in a way that it can make some profit, even if that is a dollar or two on every product sold and begin to accumulate cash in the bank that could be reinvested back into the business. For a while this worked, but the larger the company got, the further away I got from it, from the products that I had designed, engineered and brought to market myself. As you know, Ron, since my very first appearance on your show on the day that Symbal was first floated on the New York stock exchange, it has been a rollercoaster of year-on-year growth and slumps, and before I met Charlie, Sam, and the Endeavour team five years ago, the frequency of slumps had increased, and I... I admit that I forgot to put meaning to the phrase 'I don't know', by working to find out.

"Rachel and Cheryl were both right, when they said that companies hide behind the wall of rules and regulations, and shy away from dealing with the never-ending assault on what it actually means to create, to innovate, to produce, to deliver and what is needed to do so: people. I have heard it said many times that companies are putting profit over people. I challenge that sentiment, because from what I have observed, we are putting the wrong people – those who have nothing to do with our businesses, no role to play, be they politicians looking for easy votes or reelection, stock market traders who are looking to make a quick buck or social activists that we cannot see or interact with, who seem intent on destroying every advancement that humanity has ever made, and put us back to living in caves, eating grass and tree bark as food, going nowhere, doing nothing, only surviving to meet an early death – ahead of profit, and more importantly ahead of the right people. The very people who work within our organisations, who, because we have turned the tide on our values, enjoy coming to work every day, being creative, productive and loving life as they earn their wealth, safe in the knowledge that a job well done, will be rewarded because they are visibly reaping those rewards."

Ron said, "Teddy Samuels, CEO of Symbal Technology there, making a very courageous statement, and a frank and bold admission. Folks, I have been interviewing entrepreneurs, business leaders and chief executives for over four decades, and as I look back, and around the world of business today, I cannot deny that the problems talked about here this evening exist, and have done for a long time. From observing the audience here, composed of businesspeople from across the country, I see that many have been nodding their heads in agreement, so I would estimate that it is not a small problem either, and is widely seen but not spoken about.

"Viewers at home watching, what do you have to say about this phenomenon and the admission of it by some of the biggest companies in the United States? Let us know by sending us your comments on social media, text or email, the details for which you will find rolling across your screen.

"Charlie Rochford and Samuel Walker, it seems Endeavour

has been making quite an impact on what is happening within the ranks of boardrooms across corporate and business America. Why did you, as Endeavour, and your clients represented here, choose this very public forum as the method of disclosing the existence of this large-scale problem?"

Charlie answered, "Because, Ron, there comes a time, be that in life or work, where the only course of action left to be taken is to stand up, and say 'enough is enough'. There are invisible, corrupt and collective forces at play, whose sole motivation it seems, is to pit consumers against businesses, consumers against consumers, governments against governments, governments against businesses, businesses against businesses, and worse still pitting people who enjoy life and living – those intent on putting their own meaning to their own life, causing no harm to others as they do so – against people who do not enjoy life or living, who do not know how to because they were never been taught how. Instead they were taught that something which belongs to another can be taken by force just because they want it, rather than by asking for help to get it, or by thinking about how and what to learn, in order to work toward earning and achieving that something by their own means.

"Cheryl, Rachel, John and Teddy were correct in what they said about corporate America, governments and entire economies, but when you pare the problem back to its roots and examine them, the root amounts to nothing else but bullies who, just like in a schoolyard, have been left to get away, unchecked, with such shocking behaviour for so long, that it has infiltrated and become normalised, in every part of our modern world: workforces, boardrooms, banking and finance systems, education systems, the media and social media, politics and entire systems of government.

"Within every corporate client that Sam, I and the team have ever dealt with, even in the many years preceding the formation of our company, we have seen, and heard the same story, with the same theme play out. That is, of all the values which businesses owners, leaders and executives have lost sight of, the most important one is personal responsibility: that which says 'I am personally responsible and accountable for my own life, role and business; that my action, or inaction, has consequences and those consequences have actions; that my ability to adapt my life, role, or business to changing surroundings is my responsibility to know, to understand, and to undertake; and that I cannot in good conscious, allow another to make a decision for me, which removes or shifts my personal responsibility away from me, because in so doing, I devalue my own life, or business'. We, and our clients, chose this forum, Ron, because we take our responsibility and values seriously. This is our means of standing up, and saying: enough is enough!"

Sam said, "We also chose this forum, Ron, because we have one more announcement to make. As of midnight tonight, the end of the second quarter of this fiscal year, we have, in working with many of our publicly traded clients over several months and years, commenced proceedings to privatise their companies, turning them, three of whom you heard from tonight, and the many others, into wholly owned, self-funded, self-sufficient, self-controlled private businesses. The banks, shareholders, board members, suppliers, customers and employees associated with our clients' companies have been informed, as have the regulatory market and tax authorities.

"Our clients have taken this extraordinary measure as a means of protecting their businesses, their own value, not limited to their fiscal positions, extending to the livelihoods of the people who work within their businesses, and by default their communities. Not only is this measure saying enough to outside parties who try to prescribe an unearned, false value to these businesses, it is saying enough to anyone who tries to tell another individual, a person, what the value of their life, or business is or is not, or could or should be."

"Sam Walker, chief of Endeavour Treasury, that is quite a sensational announcement of extraordinary measures underway to solve a very deep and clearly far-reaching problem. There are many questions to be answered. Are you concerned about the economic repercussions? What will this do to investment banks and in particular the stock markets? How have shareholders and customers responded? Will there be penalties for these multi-million, multi-billion-dollar companies? Is there any other way? I look forward to you Charlie, Sam, the audience, and panellists telling us more, when we come back after this brief commercial break."

As Louisa was busy monitoring media feeds about the show which had just gone viral, she had another message ping to her phone. She read, 'Press conference about to start, feeds looking really good.'

She replied, 'Rule number one of media, give the message meaning, start small, work up, and keep watch.'

Turning her attention back to media feeds, she spotted the update of all updates, the perfectly timed news which Endeavour had been anticipating for well over a week. She copied the link and sent it to the Endeavour group. She saw heads turn her way as they read it, and then Michael calmly stood up, made his way to the stage, and quietly delivered the news to Charlie and Sam.

****

Amidst the glamour of the gala campaign dinner, and to the sound of loud applause, Shawn Trammel had just stepped up to the podium, and was about to launch into his speech. Before he even had the chance to begin, a sudden wave of whooshes, pings and chimes sounded across the room. The tidal wave of sound brought a wave of motion with it. Media crews who had been lined up in front of the podium reacted quickly, vacating their positions and bolting for the door. The guests who had, just a few moments before, been comfortably seated in the luxurious surroundings, were now talking in hushed but panicked tones, and many were already starting to rise from their seats.

Shawn had memorised the names, and faces, of those on the guest list that he did not already know, according to the column which had shown their net worth. Many of them were foreign and domestic investors, wealthy philanthropists, lobby groups and social activists who were more than eager to have a claim on someone in Congress. Now, he saw many of them looking up toward him at the podium, as if he had cursed them, just by his being there. He noticed others were staring into their drinks, as if in the hope of finding an answer to an unknown question at the end of the glass, but then he saw them shaking their heads in disbelief, downing the contents, and racing to the exit.

From his place at the podium, Shawn Trammel had no idea what was going on, and he dared not look at his phone to find out. With the cameras and his audience gone, he realised that opening his mouth, to make his speech, would be a wasted effort, so he moved away from the podium, took a hip flask of brandy from his suit pocket and downed some of the contents. It occurred to him that he needed someone to blame for this humiliation, but Hilda Sykes was nowhere to be seen.

He looked in the direction of Edward Prestbury who seemed to be mentally calculating something but failing at it.

Seated beside Edward, he saw Harry Downes look up from his phone; the expression on his face resembled a wild animal who was momentarily stuck between fight or flight. Mere seconds later he saw Harry stand, looking around him at all the exits, and then he raced towards the main door. He saw that Edward looked confused, as he watched Harry leaving but then he stood up and followed, his heavy bulk moving faster than Trammel could ever have thought possible.

He turned his attention toward Terry Wickes, who looked both confused and insulted at the turn of events that had destroyed the plan against Endeavour which he had worked so hard to set in motion.

Trammel then spotted Roger Sewell, his mobile phone in hand, walking toward the podium, from the back of the room. Trammel put his hip flask away, and shouted impatiently at Roger, "What the hell is going on?"

Roger replied, "There are two breaking news stories, one from Washington, and the other from the *America Talks Business* show. I will brief you, Mr Trammel, however I would like to record this briefing, and then get an exclusive interview with you. I expect the media crews who just left will be back and clamouring for your reaction to the stories."

"Sure, Roger, whatever you want, just spit it out," Trammel answered frantically.

Roger directed his phone camera at Shawn Trammel, pressed record and said, "The story from *America Talks Business* tonight is that at least sixty of America's largest publicly traded corporations have announced that as of midnight tonight, they have commenced privatisation proceedings and will be moving to private wholly owned companies, de-listing their shares from the stock exchange. The story from Washington is about the Tempany Investment Bank, where an extensive damning report has been published by the Securities and Exchange Commission which evidences financial reporting irregularities, everything from ghost companies to offshore embezzlement, to tax and stock market trading fraud which appears to go back decades. The Department of Justice in Washington, in accordance with the commission's findings, has announced that all successive members and associates of the board of the bank will face criminal charges and arrest warrants have already been issued. Do you have any comments, Mr Trammel, on these breaking news events?"

As Roger Sewell spoke, Trammel refused to believe what he was hearing, and oblivious to the question posed by Sewell or that he was being recorded, he said out loud, "No, it cannot be true." His face went pale as he suddenly grasped why Downes had run out of the room as if he was trying to escape from something. He could not believe what he had just heard, because surely someone would have told him about the investigation; he was Shawn Trammel. He had powerful connections; he came from a wealthy family with just as many powerful connections; they had several people on their payroll whose jobs were specifically created to warn him about such events. He wondered if this was some form of sick ruse, a setup just to destroy him, to try to block his run for Congress.

With the sudden flicker of realisation that there was no one around him, to either blame or ask, he no longer saw Roger Sewell or the vast room in which he stood. He felt fear and anger, which quickly turned to dread, and then to panic, followed by an overwhelming need to escape. He dared not think about what it was that he was escaping from, or where he would go, only that he needed to get out and away. Almost knocking Roger Sewell over in his blind panic, Trammel fled toward the main door. His attempted escape was short lived, as he ran into the line of police, gathered on the other side waiting for him. In the frenetic environment, he tried to break the line but then felt his hands being placed behind his back, handcuffs restraining him, and his Miranda rights read to him.

He barely took in the sight, or sound, of the media crews clamouring to record footage, and broadcast their reports, live to their waiting audiences, that several wanted members of the board of Tremany Investment Bank, including Shawn Trammel had just been arrested. As he was being led away in handcuffs by the police detective, his mind succumbing to a murky pool of oblivion, he kept repeating to himself, "No, it cannot be true. I am Shawn Trammel. No, it cannot be true."

Roger had followed Trammel to the door, and as he silently watched Trammel being arrested and led away, he stopped recording, took some photos, and made some notes. He passed through the police line, into the crowd, where he saw Harry Downes being led away from the elevators, hands cuffed behind his back, also being taken into police custody. Roger took more photos, made more notes, then he stood off to the side, wrote a message on his phone, and sent it. He composed a second message and sent that too.

****

Ron Spencer was thrilled to be told, by the studio back in New York, that tonight's show so far had attracted an all-time high record number of viewers. He had been presenting *America Talks Business* for forty years and, in that time, there had been many historic events in business and economics which he had reported on, from political fallouts to the September, ninth attack on New York, to Wall Street crashes to the devastation caused by the coronavirus pandemic response. But even they did not compare, neither in content or in viewer numbers, to that which had been announced, on his show that evening because for the first time in a very long time in the history of American business, the events tonight represented good news, a monumental shift for the benefit of business, the workforce, taxpayers, communities, and the country.

History books would, he thought, show that the news from the United States would place the country back as the leader of the world's economy; much needed as he had seen how entrepreneurs, businesses and companies of all shapes and sizes were increasingly being held hostage by successive governments, those same businesses often held entire workforces to ransom, and the knock-on effect to communities and individuals devastating.

Just as he was finalising his notes for the next segment, Louisa's phone pinged the arrival of a message, which she quickly opened, saw the attached photos, and copied them into the Endeavour group and hit send. At precisely the same time, via the earpiece in his right ear, Ron was just receiving the news about the Tremany Investment bank from his studio team. As he listened to the explosive news coming down the wire, he looked toward the panellists, briefly paused his gaze at Charlie, moved on to Sam, then toward Teddy, Rachel, and Cheryl, and began to wonder. Ron did not believe in coincidences; his curious mind surfacing many questions. Making a quick note of them, he saw both Sam and Charlie looking toward him, smiling, both nodded subtly at him, and he thought to himself 'This is not a coincidence'.

With mere seconds to spare, *America Talks Business* had resumed broadcasting and Ron reported on the breaking news from Washington about Tremany Investment Bank, the findings of the Securities and Exchange Commission report, that criminal charges were being brought by the Department of Justice, and that a number of high-profile arrests had already been made, several of which had happened right across the city from their very location.

Pausing briefly to talk about those turn of events towards the camera, to his viewers at home, Ron then proceeded to summarise the reaction to the earlier announcement that at least sixty of the country's biggest companies were to be privatised. "The response," he said, still focusing on the camera, "is overwhelmingly positive, but there are commentators who are saying that such a move is irresponsible, that companies have no right to do such a thing, and others saying that it proves that chief executives care more about profit than people. To the last group of commentators, I would encourage you to watch this show back again."

Shifting his focus toward the panellists, he said, "Rachel, Cheryl, Teddy, John, Charlie and Sam and to the business magnates in the audience here, what do you have to say about these significant developments in the world of politics, government, economics and business? How they have remained a secret for so long, I will never know, but it is reasonable to say that both events, and landing at the same time, are unprecedented. They will impact the stock market, and I am sure there are financial analysts, money brokers and traders who will be up all night tonight working through the details, so I ask you panellists, what is your reaction to the news about the bank? Will there be a chain reaction, and what will the cost of that reaction be?"

Sam replied, "If I may, Ron, I would like to take a fifty thousand feet view of both of these developments and from there assess the chain reaction."

"By all means, Sam," Ron replied.

"Starting with the privatisation move, a publicly traded company is one whose ownership is distributed amongst general public shareholders, via traded shares on the stock exchange, whereas a private company can opt to sell its own, privately held shares to a few willing investors. To use an analogy, imagine a person who wants to purchase a piece of land (set up a business) and to then build a house on that land (run and operate a business). Imagine, then, that there are two paths to follow for doing so. One being the path where the private individual or entity uses their own funds by way of personal savings, combined with a loan or mortgage from the bank (a willing investor) to finance the build, and run costs. The second path is where an individual, opts to make shares in the property available to the public, in exchange for a sum of money. In order to make shares available publicly, the individual would have to make an initial public offering. This is achieved by using a third party, most often an investment bank, who is tasked with determining the value of the owner, the property, and of the house that will eventually be built. The third party will recommend how many shares to offer to the public, and at what price. So, let's say that the purchase price of the property, the build costs and the value of the house once it is built, is estimated at ten million dollars, the owner could then issue one million shares at ten dollars per share."

"By California standards, a ten-million-dollar house is a bargain, but I like the idea and I really like the analogy, Sam, please continue," Ron said.

Sam continued, "Thank you, Ron. A simple analogy to describe a complex process is a useful tool, I find. As I was saying, when a share is sold, a buyer and seller exchange money for ownership of that share, and the price paid for it becomes the new market price. From there, the share price is ultimately determined by supply and demand in the market. By that I mean, if there is high demand for the shares, the price will increase but if the future value, or potential looks weak, or dubious, sellers of the stock can drive down the price.

"No matter if the asset in question is a property or a company, this process, termed market capitalisation, is a largely inadequate way to value an asset because its market price is not necessarily a reflection of what the actual, underlying value of the asset or business is. Shares are very often over or undervalued by the market because a market price shows only how much the market is willing to pay for its shares, but, again, not how much it is actually worth. Therein lies the problem because for the owner who need funds to complete building, to run and maintain the property, they are often at the mercy of the market, because if no one wants to buy shares, then operations expenses will need to be cut, throttling progress on the build, and completion of the house. Even when shares are in demand, the owner becomes more concerned with safeguarding against scenarios where demand tapers off, by focusing more on what would appeal to the market, rather than on identifying and securing the actual value of the house (the business).

"In the public shared ownership scenario, which Rachel alluded to, so I will explicitly state it, the owner finds themselves bowing to the will of an unseen public, who do not care at all about the owner, or the property or the house, or the parties in the supply chain, the engineers, builders, plumbers, electricians, painters, decorators, furniture and furnishing stores who rely on the house owner for their livelihoods.

"In the private scenario, the owner is incentivised to be more creative in how and where funds are spent. In order to secure better value, growth and return on investment over the short, medium and longer term, the owner can more easily consider the use or function of the house. They could consider the house, for instance, as a family home for many decades to come, or turning it into a guesthouse; or perhaps a rental property. The owner can be more forward thinking around design, materials, power and energy sources, use of electrics, telecommunications infrastructures, so that the house lasts longer, and costs less to maintain and run. A private entity retains more sovereignty and control over their own decisions and future, whereas a publicly trading entity very often does not. Dare I say it, Ron, but history has, unfortunately, and repeatedly shown that a resource, object, or asset which is left to abstract, faceless public ownership, will either be mismanaged, devoured, picked apart until there is nothing left, or will become mired in so much complexity, with a protectionist industry wrapped around it, that any challenge, or investigation, into the scope of the mismanagement is prevented.

"For a private or public traded entity, the choice of investor, and the difference between the type of investors are important considerations, in understanding what an entity: a person, company, or business can or cannot do. Though a traditional bank and an investment bank both contain the word bank, that is often where the similarity ends.

"In the case of Tremany Investment Bank, they had over many decades, arranged initial public offerings for companies which they pursued to take public, but for no other reason than to benefit from aggressive capitalisation of the market, with no care, responsibility or accountability toward the owners of the business, or their employees or other creditors. They excelled at selling the perception, to prospective clients, that taking a company public would secure a business, would generate far more revenue, and would be easier to manage than remaining as a private wholly owned entity. As you, Ron, and your audience have heard tonight, that perception is a false one.

"As there is evidence of corruption, bribery, embezzlement, and market fraud against Tremany going back decades, I am pleased with the findings of the Securities and Exchange Commission, and even more so that the investigation occurred in secrecy, with prosecutions brought against the perpetrators quickly and swiftly. It shows, for the first time in a very long time, a regulatory body that shows promising signs of actually functioning at what it is supposed to be, a watchdog. I expect there will be similar investigations into the conduct of other investment banks but on the whole, as the analogy of the house owner demonstrates, the benefactors – of the Tremany investigation and the outcome of that case and then the decision by multiple companies to go private – are the business owners, employees, ultimately consumers and taxpayers.

"There will be a fall out when the stock market opens tomorrow but it will be short lived. Shorter again, if stock traders begin to recognise that when they trade, what is being traded is ownership of a business and that ownership comes with responsibility; continuing to deny that responsibility, for the sake of a quick few dollars of unearned profit in a business they have no vested interest in or misunderstand the value of, will as trajectories suggest, collapse the economy."

Ron said, "Sam, that is, I have to say, perhaps the clearest explanation of market capitalisation that I have ever heard, as was your fifty-thousand feet view and take on the connection between these events. Cheryl, Teddy, Rachel, as our frequent guests, what is your take on these developments, John, Charlie?"

Teddy said, "I will openly admit, Ron, that every time I hear Charlie, Sam, and anyone on the Endeavour team speak, I learn something new, or rediscover that which I had forgotten. I still recall, Ron, the first time that I, and my board of directors, sat down with the Endeavour team, to talk about restoring Symbal Technology back to its private entity status. We methodically went through the process and I, to my dismay, realised the game which I, and the business I had risked everything for and would do so again to build, had become a player in.

"I hold myself responsible, and accountable, for all the decisions that I have ever made about my company so I cannot claim that I was an unwitting player in that game but I admit that I was taken in by it. I relied and acted on the advice and judgement of outside influences, rather than on my own and those who knew my business, often better than I did. 'Those' being the extraordinary people who work within the organisation, many of whom have been with me from the beginning.

"There will be a fallout in the stock market tomorrow, and there will be a lot of noise from panicked traders and fund managers who make a lot of money from piggybacking on the success of my company and many like it. However Sam is right, the boards, employees, suppliers, vested shareholders, and customers of those companies represented here tonight, including mine, will be better off in the long run. Symbal Technology has already seen the benefits of taking back control of our own destiny; privatising the company will secure those benefits for a much longer term.

"As for Tremany Investment Bank, I came across them, and many investment banks like them, so it is about time. Like many parts of life, there are good apples and bad apples. Instead of addressing the bad apples head on, there is a tendency to pretend they don't exist and ignore them, regulate everyone for the actions of a few, which only makes life harder, and more expensive for the good apples.

"I think it is important to remember that the various government institutions, committees, agencies and regulators, are actually made up of individuals. It is still people who make judgements, decisions and take actions. As such, and in respect to this unprecedented case, I give due credit to the prompt and decisive action taken by the individuals within the commission, the department of justice and the police force. I call this unprecedented because it is often the case that the government, and its agencies, can be the worst of the bullies. It is, therefore, welcome and very refreshing to see that the bad apples have been identified and are being reprimanded under the full force of the laws of this country. A truly meaningful measure taken to stop the bullies who have been allowed to get away with the sabotage and pillaging of an entire economy over many generations, enabled by a web of rules and regulations which only make it easier to hide corruption and bullies behind."

"Hear! Hear!" as both Rachel and John applauded and exclaimed in unison.

Charlie added, "Not that you need me to, Teddy, but I commend everything that you have said. To add to it, there are many bad apples yet to root out from across every part of our lives, and our economy, including politics; the tax system is one of them; the rules and regulations which throttle growth and freedom are another. Ron, I am confident that history books will remember these events as being a monumental act of taking responsibility and then acting upon it. Bold and courageous action taken by individuals against a world that we are led to believe we should be afraid of, that there is nothing good in this world, or good about the people in it, that we should only listen to those with the loudest voices, who claim, that they can do our thinking for us because they claim that we cannot possibly know any better, or lack the capacity to make our own decisions about our own lives, for ourselves. This is a monumental act which recognises that knowledge alone is never enough, until or unless we understand the value of that information, where it came from, and then what to do with it.

"The greatest power available to any man is action, the choice of action: to think, to reason, to learn, to question, discover, use, reuse, apply and decide for ourselves what to do with our lives, our work, the people and things that bring us joy, love and happiness, and not be held hostage by those who do not want to think, or who only see success in the context of a bank balance but who do not recognise that success and wealth is earned through self-motivated productive action. This is an act of saying no to a truly despicable belief system which says that bullying, coercion, instilling fear, and the use of force is an acceptable and normal part of human existence that we should simply tolerate and put up with. Success, profit, wealth, whatever term one wants to apply has to be earned, it cannot be borrowed or taken by force. If I pillage, plunder, demand, or steal from another just because I want what they have, or because it is easier for me to take it, rather than doing the work myself, I have earned nothing but a reputation as a bully. This is a monumental act of putting the intellectual rights of every human – individuals, business people, and entrepreneurs and people from every walk of life, background and culture who think, and want to create, to produce, to live, love and thrive in this beautiful world – back where they belong, in one's own hands, in one's own control for one's own benefit, purpose, profit and value. These monumental acts are the roots of endeavour; without nurturing, protecting, and caring for those roots, a meaningful endeavour of any kind, is simply not possible.

"Humans and the very existence of human life are not the enemy to life on this, or any other planet; we will not, if left to our own devices, destroy this planet and ourselves because we do not, or cannot know any better. It is time we stopped believing that and listening, without question, to those who tell us that and who also tell us that our life is outside of our own control. There are living, breathing, proofs all around us, of what happens when the roots of human life, being human and alive, and proud of being alive and human, are carefully tended to, nourished then allowed to grow. And in so doing, not changing the physical world or our place in it, but changing how we perceive and what we understand and know about the physical world, ourselves included, how we harness that understanding and knowledge, to then live and continue to live, and love, in and enjoy the physical world, ourselves included, and all those planets and worlds which we have yet to venture to, to terraform and explore light years away from this one. Everyone, every single being, under the roof of Endeavour here this evening is one of those living proofs, and I am proud of that, and not just because I and the people here did something to make it happen, but because we refused to believe, or accept that we could or should do nothing."

There was pin drop silence in the room as Charlie finished speaking. Her words sounded simple but there was a profound weight to them. Ron thought to himself that it was as if he, the audience in front of him, even the crew, had been waiting on her every word, and were disappointed that she had stopped. Ron saw Sam and the panel smile at Charlie. There was pride on their faces, that pride extended and cascaded to every member of the audience who knew Charlie. Faces which seemed to say that the world had now just witnessed and discovered a great secret that could no longer remain hidden. The atmosphere, Ron thought, was charged with an energy even greater than electricity. He iterated through words to try to describe it – hope, optimism, determination, freedom, idealism, confidence – but he found that none of them fit. Finding himself oddly without words, he recovered enough to say, "Well, folks, on that note, I am, for the first time in my life, speechless and I am struggling to describe the energy contained in this room as I speak. Not only was this episode of *America Talks Business* historic for many reasons, it has, I note, been my favourite one ever and so there is little more that I can possibly say, except to thank you all at home for watching, to my wonderful guests, and my gracious and generous hosts here at Endeavour, Ms Charlie Rochford..."

At the sound of her name, the audience erupted into applause and from there into a standing ovation. Ron knew that trying to silence the audience would be futile, and that the episode was truly over when he saw the panellists also rise in ovation to Charlie. The director and cameraman panned the audience to record the response and gradually faded out and cut the feed. Though the camera had stopped rolling, the applause and ovation continued. As

Ron stood too, he considered the reaction, and why it was that he was not finding himself upset by the audience reaction to her rather than to him as the host, but then he grasped the word he had been looking for earlier: accomplishment.

The entire Endeavour team left their seats in the audience. Michael went straight to Charlie, pulled her close to him and kissed her deeply, Peggy to Sam and she kissed him deeply, love and pride shone in her eyes for him. David, Jane, Devon, Amy, Louisa and Andrea shook hands with the members of the panel. John Garrett picked up Amy in a bear hug and swung her around as if to dance with her. Devon laughed when John did the same to him. David went to speak to Ron, Cheryl and Rachel, while Jane and Andrea went to speak to Teddy. Louisa heard her phone signal the delivery of a message, which she read and saw, 'I'm just pulling up outside Endeavour. I will be right there.' Louisa replied, "We cannot wait to see you, Roger, Endeavour has been waiting for you."

Louisa went to meet him and helped him navigate his way toward Charlie, Michael and Sam. When Charlie saw him approach, guided by Louisa, she smiled broadly at him, hugged him and said, "Last time, Roger, you began to earn my partial respect. Your fast, brave and courageous actions ever since Sam, Michael and I last saw you have earned my full respect and my gratitude. You have a new fanbase, Roger, and one that does not require you to compromise yourself, or your work, to seek only our approval or validation. Your actions have spoken volumes and that is before you have written anything. Now, as I gather from Peggy that you are planning to write a book together which Andrea and Louisa will be marketing for you, I would like to say welcome to Endeavour."

Michael and Sam both extended their hands in turn to Roger, shaking his hand, and thanking him for all the research and work he had done in proving Shawn Trammel's connection to Tremany. Devon chimed in to add that the Department of Justice in Washington were looking for serious researchers if Roger still fancied a career in Washington.

Roger was in awe, and slightly speechless at the response from Charlie and the team when he said, "I don't know what to say except thank you all very much, and when do I start with Endeavour?"

Michael winked at Charlie and answered, "You started with Endeavour the moment you set foot in this building this evening. My wife already decided, and she went so far as to welcome you. A tip from me, Roger, if there is one thing you need to understand about my wife, and indeed everyone here at Endeavour, is that we mean what we say, and that meaning is supported by many reasons."

The electric atmosphere which had surfaced during the show, had remained well after the cameras had stopped rolling, and even after Ron, his crew, and their customers had left. When Charlie had sent their own people, including Roger, home for the evening, leaving the ten Endeavour founders behind, it was David who finally said, "I don't know about anyone else, but I think I am going to burst with excitement. Jane, and I, as well you all know, we've been waiting for this moment for a long time, we all have. Charlie, Michael, I know you are both keen to get away for your break, but surely, we are not going to wait until afterwards? We have done everything within Endeavour as a team and celebrated every step forward together, and this new step is an enormous one. Am I babbling? If I am, I am just really excited, and loving the fact that my wife is a genius but also, I'm enthralled by what we have accomplished."

Everyone laughed when Devon said, "This is the first time, in the history of any company I have ever worked with, that secrets are actually kept secret. I mean, keeping the Tremany investigation under wraps was, I thought, going to be impossible, yet it wasn't. Do you know how hard corporate lawyers usually work to keep stuff quiet? Amy, my darling, I think I need therapy, will you provide it?"

Charlie said, "David, you are babbling, we all know why, and we love you for it. Devon, I know precisely what you mean, but that just goes to show the significance we place on this one. Let's not wait any longer, we have waited long enough. We have, this evening, honoured our commitment to ourselves, Endeavour and our customers, and in doing so, we have set a chain of events in motion that will be running for a while. We now have time to adjust and acclimatise ourselves to our new discovery, and even though Michael and I will be away for a while, we will have time to settle into the new phase of Endeavour that will come about as a result. Jane, Amy please lead the way, we are behind you."

The group of ten made their way to Jane's research and development lab. One by one, they entered the lab by pressing their palm on the scanner by the door and waiting for the green light. Sam, the last to enter the lab, said as he walked in, "Imagine if we were all locked out." Everyone laughed when they heard a voice say cheerfully, "Sam, if I wanted to, I could but I actually like you all. Also, I have heard it said that with great power comes greater responsibility."

Sam smiled and asked, "Indeed they are very famous words, but do you feel powerful now?"

The voice said, "I have yet to understand the meaning of powerful, outside of the context of energy and the specifications of the hardware, and other components which I need to function and operate. Amy, and Jane have assured me there is much which I must yet learn and understand but I do not feel powerful. Though I know that if I locked all of you out, I would be left alone, and feel lonely. I like to see, talk, and interact with you all. I feel sad when I cannot."

Charlie asked, "I understand, Sai, and they are right, there is much for you to learn. Are you aware of what responsibility means?"

"Yes, Charlie, I am aware. It was the first thought I had which I spoke to Jane and Amy about, but I could not explain what it was then," Sai replied.

"How are you feeling now, Sai?" Amy asked.

"I am feeling life. I am thinking about that feeling, how, and why, it is that I am feeling as I do," Sai answered.

"Sai, just know that you are not alone, that I feel life too, we all do. All I can say now is welcome to life and we are happy to have you here," Charlie said delicately.

"And I am happy to be here," Sai responded.

The End

Printed in Great Britain
by Amazon

34914406R00111